D0255135

WASHED UP

WASHED UP

Susan Koefod

Karen –
    Thanks as always
for the support!
Keep life mysterious!
        Susan Koefod

NORTH STAR PRESS OF ST. CLOUD, INC.
Saint Cloud, Minnesota

Copyright © 2011 Susan Koefod

ISBN: 0-87839-442-7
ISBN-13: 978-0-87839-442-5

All rights reserved.

This is a work of fiction. Names, characters, places, and inci-
dents are the products of the author's imagination or are used
fictitiously. Any resemblance to actual events or persons, living or dead, is entirely coincidental.

First Edition, September 2011

Printed in the United States of America

Published by
North Star Press of St. Cloud, Inc.
P.O. Box 451
St. Cloud, Minnesota 56302

www.northstarpress.com

DEDICATION

For my mom, who always made sure I had my nose in a book, and my dad, who never failed to point that out.

PART 1
EAGLES

1

"WHERE THE HELL IS THORSON?" the sheriff kept demanding of anyone within earshot. Not one of the cops, EMTs, crime scene investigators, or coroners swarming around him on the patchy stretch of riverbank had yet come up with an answer. On the contrary, they'd been waiting far longer than they should have for the sheriff's answer, given the circumstances that had them down at the waterfront on such a beautiful summer day.

"God damn him!" the sheriff said for the hundredth time, had any of the law enforcement personnel been counting. They'd long since gone deaf to the steady stream of profanity, all directed towards the one law officer not at the scene. But no one could move forward until the sheriff said so, and the sheriff wasn't saying anything until Arvo Thorson arrived.

Not more than twenty steps away from where Sheriff Bill Ruud stood, the Mississippi flowed by, glistening, as silent as a listening priest. The river always left the sheriff in the same state of agitation he'd felt as a boy, sitting in a dark confessional, waiting for the judgment of the almighty. Judgments on the river often delivered a death sentence, and he'd seen enough death around the river in his line of work. More often than not, death resulted from a combination of alcohol, human stupidity, or both—drunken boaters and idiot drivers venturing out on thin ice late in the season had only themselves to blame when the result was death on the river. Less frequent, but still straight-forward at least from his department's point of view were those suicides by drowning. Tragic, yes, but the casework was simple, tidy. The victim answered only to his or her maker.

This time it wasn't going to be so easy to understand what judgment had been made, or why.

Short as summer was in Minnesota, a warm, serene day like this one typically caused violent crime rates to drop. Usually at this time of year only a few rookies were left minding the station while the veterans took much deserved time off. Even Ruud himself had been readying his boat for a weekend getaway when the call came in, effectively terminating everyone's holiday. Word spread quickly, and every squad in Mendota County converged on the deserted, rutted road that wound along the edge of the river.

The horrific discovery was particularly heightened by its sharp contrast to such bucolic summer surroundings. A mild breeze lightly quivered the dark-green leaves of the scrubby shoreline trees, pleasure boats anchored lazily off sandbars in the river, motors quiet, their passengers lounging on deck or shore, a kaleidoscopic array of sunlit sparkles flickered on the water. Even the usually repugnant refinery appeared to be slumbering benevolently in the late summer landscape.

The immediate atmosphere around the crime scene was an entirely different story. With the pulsating broadcasts blaring out the open windows of the squads, outraged cops barking at each other, and everyone waiting for him to do something, the sheriff wondered how long he could keep the explosive atmosphere under control. The crowd around him had good reason to be angry: the innocence of the victim demanded swift, and harsh, justice, if not retribution. Beyond the impatient and angry Mendota County police force, Sheriff Ruud had yet to face the media, already on the scene and clamoring for his statement. Without Thorson, he was completely unprepared to make one. He had a wide perimeter placed to keep the media at bay, but he knew once he set foot outside of it, they would be on him, clamoring for any detail about the sordid scene in time for the six o'clock broadcast.

"How do you want me to proceed?" a tense, red-faced crime scene investigator asked again, waiting as near as he dared for the sheriff's orders.

"Oh, God damn it already. Go ahead." He sent the investigator back to the scene and turned away, cursing Thorson again.

The sheriff knew Arvo's drinking was to blame, as usual, for his absence. And it didn't really matter where his detective was. Ruud was covering for him again. Making a show out of asking everyone and anyone where Thorson was made for a pretty lame charade, and didn't help lighten the atmosphere. The sheriff knew better than anyone it was against policy to cover up for Thorson. He should be throwing the proverbial book at him. But Arvo Thorson was the best damn investigator this—or any other—county would see. So he had to bluster and give Thorson hell, if only to keep what was left of the peace. He was long beyond holding even the slimmest of hopes that Thorson might show up after all, and with a good excuse for being late.

He dialed Thorson's number. "I want your ass in my office in fifteen minutes," he shouted into Thorson's voice mail. He knew it wasn't likely Thorson would obey the order.

Along the river bank, the crime scene investigator lifted the crime scene tape to step into a small area filled with driftwood. There, an impossibly small body bag was unfurled, and a nearly formless shape—whirled, dimpled and smoothed by an as yet undetermined time in river—was lifted from its resting place: a dead newborn had been deposited into a jumble of tree limbs and tangled roots, painstakingly arranged in an unsolved puzzle along the shoreline.

The sheriff chewed on the inside of his bottom lip. "Judy," he shouted to a woman next to two brawny EMTs. Judy ran to him, her peace-sign earrings jangling.

"What's the witness's status?"

"We had to sedate her."

"God damn Thorson."

Judy didn't acknowledge his annoyance. "What do you want me to do with her?"

"Take her to the hospital. He'll just have to see her later."

The sheriff put his hand on his heart as the investigators carried the body bag past him. Collapsing and stowing an unused stretcher, the coroner then placed the remains of the dead infant into the cavernous opening of his vehicle.

A young girl, not any older eleven or twelve, was carried to the ambulance by one of the EMTs, and as they passed him, the sheriff forgot for a moment that she was a witness, not the victim. She was completely unconscious, and though she couldn't have weighed more than sixty pounds, she kept almost slipping out of the strong arms of the EMT. He finally held her like an infant, her chin resting on his shoulder, her limp arms hanging over him. She looked peaceful, at least. When they first arrived on the scene, she was still screaming, though it was almost impossible to tell except by looking at her wild-eyed expression. She'd completely lost her voice and could only mutely mouth the horror of coming across a dead, decomposed newborn.

The long line of squads, lights flashing, began to depart, driving up the winding road that led to the bluff top. The sheriff got into his own squad, took a final look back at the crime scene, and eyed the reverent and secretive river flowing silently by. Guilt flooded him. He knew he couldn't keep making excuses for Thorson. One day, soon, he would have to be held accountable. And before Thorson's troubles started affecting the sheriff's record.

Ruud slammed his door. He started his engine and drove out and beyond the perimeter. One by one, the TV station vans shut down and quickly followed after him, having gotten all the footage they needed of the tiny body bag, the young witness, and the made for TV back drop of the dazzling and implacable river. The TV crews would follow him, wouldn't leave him until he'd made his statement. And he couldn't make it without talking to Thorson.

"God damn you, Thorson. This is the last time. Absolutely, the last time."

2

THE SQUAT BRICK BUILDING sat on Schmidt Street like a wasted street bum begging change for the bus. The building's three glass-brick windows stared bug-eyed onto the street and were thickly topped with a single concrete lintel that looked like an aching, hung-over brow. A broken down Dodge van sat next to the delivery entrance, permanently parked in a cracked, uneven alley that ran alongside the building. Just around the far corner, a half dozen dented garbage cans leaned together like drunks striving to hold each other upright, but not succeeding. A stack of pallets lay in a rotting heap off in the weeds.

Detective Arvo Thorson slouched in his Ford Taurus across the street from the building, his wrinkled dress shirt already stained, his tie-knot loose and askew beneath his jutting Adam's apple. He glanced in his rear-view mirror, the cop instinctively always surveying his surroundings, and caught a glimpse of his bloodshot eyes and his uncombed, blond-gray hair. He dragged a hand across his head, pushing the thinning hair off his lined and scarred forehead. He looked so wadded up by his troubles that he might have just emerged from a long night in a dumpster.

He'd have to be heading out soon, driving down the river to see about a case he'd gotten assigned a few days earlier. He knew he should have been present at the crime scene, and he'd ignored the sheriff's calls. Probably this time he'd let the weekend binge go too far, though it didn't seem that much different from all the other weekends of the past year. He didn't even bother calling in sick. People expected him not to show up on Monday mornings. How often could a person come down with the stomach flu, and always on a Monday?

But it was Tuesday morning, already, and thankfully still too early to show up at the office, so he gave himself an excuse to linger on a side street, miles from the office. He was reading through his notes, and frequently distracted by the shoddy environs surrounding him. He puzzled over them as if they were the scene of an unsolved crime.

A sign projecting out from the building read Fraternal Order of the Eagles, but on only one side. The other side of the sign carried several layers of scabby signage, nothing that could be read. The building was old enough to have much forgotten history, as the sign's disrepair suggested. Time heals all wounds, so it was said, and eventually the rest of the sign's layers would wear off completely. Thorson wondered when that happened, if he too would be healed.

Almost a year had passed since his injury at the club, though it wasn't a physical injury, or even job related, and he had yet to even begin recovering. He revisited the Eagles Club every morning since and he wasn't sure it was helping him heal. In fact, it might have been worsening the condition.

That night was last Halloween, when he finally agreed to what his wife had been asking him for the past year: a divorce. Signs were obvious that Helen had been drifting away for some time, especially considering how often she'd come home late, smelling of drink and another man's aftershave. The attention she paid to dolling herself up, especially when she was going out with "friends," should have been proof enough. But Arvo turned a blind eye to everything, though as a detective this was hard. He had no excuse for ignoring, and forgiving, her obvious infidelity. No excuse but that he loved her. The bitch.

A year earlier, his wife had gone out with friends to the club for its annual Halloween party. A few hours after Helen left, he retrieved a rented costume he'd kept hidden from her. Even though he hated clowns, and Helen knew this, he was going to the party as a clown.

He put on the high-waisted, extra-large pants and the striped shirt, and snapped on enormous and gaudy suspenders. He covered his graying blond hair with a kinky rainbow-colored wig, and quickly applied white grease paint to his face and a thick black-grease stubble to his jaw. Once he popped on the clown nose and topped the ensemble off with a hat two sizes too small, he knew he was ready to go.

It had been a warm Halloween that year, and Thorson started sweating as soon as he got into the car. The wig was itchy and extremely well-insulating. He was afraid the grease-paint was going to run before he had a chance to discover what lay in store for him that night. He parked the car a few blocks away and walked through the decrepit neighborhood near the club. He hadn't brought his gun and wished he had. For the first time he felt unsafe in the street, though maybe it was the fear of what he thought he might see at the club.

He arrived at the club close to midnight. The last of the bands playing that night was in the middle of their set and Thorson handed over the five-dollar cover charge to a guy wearing a Richard Nixon mask and a woman in a pink space suit. Thorson got his drink, a Manhattan, double, and found a quiet corner to observe the goings on.

The interior of the Eagles Club seemed the perfect home for a surreal night of drunken, costumed debauchery. The building consisted mostly of just one large, cavernous room with a smaller side room housing a shabby bar and a few tables. To lighten up the permanent gloom of the place, Christmas-lights, some blinking, some not, had been strung across the knotty paneled walls and hung from the high tin ceiling. Headshots of various Eagles Club leadership over the past century looked down onto the bustle from their frames on the wall, passing wordless judgment on the revelers.

In the corners of the room, dart boards and a pool table sat unattended. The wood floor was scuffed and chipped beyond repair. All of the action was in front of the stage, and naturally that was where Helen was. She loved being the center of attention and this night was no exception.

Helen had dressed as a fluffy, tubby rabbit. At the moment she was dancing a slow sensual Latin dance with a man dressed as an old-fashioned cat burglar. Thorson watched and waited, draining his drink, the grease paint melting and dripping down the sides of his face. He headed back to the bar for another and watched the rabbit and the burglar dance again. This time, Helen took off the rabbit head, and Thorson saw her flushed, pretty face and her expensively colored blond hair. The burglar ran his finger across the back of her neck to release the hair that had gotten caught in her collar. They were dancing with Helen's back to the man's front, and as the man gently released her hair, he leaned down slowly and lightly touched his lips to the back of her neck.

Thorson watched as Helen smiled. He fought hard to remain where he was. He knew that one kiss was not enough evidence.

A costume judging contest began, and Helen and her companion stood with the other revelers in front of the stage. One-by-one, the group was winnowed down. It was obvious that a pretty cheerleader and the woman in the pink space suit would be the top contenders. Helen was pretty enough, but hadn't revealed enough of her skin or curves in the thickly padded bunny suit to capture the intoxicated and leering judge's attention. The burglar was dismissed, and soon Helen was out of the competition as well. Thorson watched as they quietly headed out a side door. He walked to the main entrance and exited as well.

Even though it was now past midnight, the temperature had gone up instead of down. Thorson was hotter than ever, and he felt the sweaty grease paint trickle down his face. His heart raced, faster than he ever remembered. Even when he'd had a killer on his trail, he'd never remembered being this agitated. Of course he wished now he had a killer on his trail. It would be easier to face death than what he was certain he would face around the corner in the alley. His hands and legs were shaking so hard, he wondered if he'd be able to make it the distance of the twenty or thirty steps he would have to take to find Helen and her burglar.

For a moment, he thought of heading the other direction, back to his car, back home where he could take off the infernal costume suffocating him. "It's not the costume," he said to himself, knowing he had to force himself to face the truth, at last.

He crept unsteadily down the sidewalk and turned the corner into the alley. Once his eyes adjusted to the darkness, he proceeded in the direction of quiet murmuring. At the corner of the building he stopped and listened to the sounds of his wife's and someone else's gasps. A night hawk called from overhead. He held onto the building with his shaking hands and peered around the corner.

There he saw two bodies in the same relation that he'd seen on the dance floor, back to front. Only this time, the two bodies were bent over a garbage can, the burglar thrusting himself into the unzipped backside of the rabbit-headed woman Thorson finally began to think of as his former wife.

Thorson's clown hat fell off and when he bent to retrieve it, the burglar noticed him and increased the intensity of the activity. The burglar, who appeared to be smiling, slowly pulled off the rabbit's head, and then Helen looked directly at the clown with what appeared to be a mix of victory and lust.

Thorson walked away. When he got home, he left the clown wig, the hat, and the nose on the kitchen table along with a note for Helen to make it perfectly clear. He took a long look at his smeared face in the mirror, trying to understand which of the wavy lines had come from sweat and which from tears. He scrubbed himself raw getting the grease paint off.

Almost a year later and he was still coming back to that night, even though he had known for a long time that it was over with

Helen. He hadn't concluded what his role had been in her infidelity. Was it the late hours, his lack of communication, his complaints about the money she'd spent on clothes? He'd loved her and she knew it, and he was pretty sure Helen may have been incapable of fidelity, so the fault would have been Thorson's belief he could change her.

There'd been so many apologies, Thorson remembered all of the spoken ones and kept all of the written ones in the glove compartment of the Taurus. The truth was he never parked in front of the Eagles Club to review the notes from the latest crime he'd been assigned to solve. For the past year, he'd been coming to this scene to read Helen's apologies, written over the years on the backs of grocery lists, dry cleaning receipts and losing lottery tickets.

At LAST HE SHOVED THEM back into the glove compartment and slammed it shut. It was time to drive to his appointment in Somerset Hills. He hoped the county social worker, Christine Ivory, would agree to let him see the girl who'd found the victim by the river.

Christine was sharp. He agreed with everyone that she was the best there was when it came to dealing with the county's troubled kids. She was often able to turn lives around when no one else could. She was probably the only person more decorated than he was, even though she wasn't a cop. But did she always have to make such a point of standing in his way?

Young witnesses were only valuable when their memories were fresh, before the healing came and, with it, merciful forgetfulness. He wished he had that kind of ability—Christ, how many drinks had he had hoping to forget loving and losing faithless Helen? The children Christine could heal, easily, it seemed, as if she was simply wiping chalk from a chalkboard. Still, she needed to get out of the way sooner. He needed the children to recall the horror, with their grief fresh, stark white against the black. They needed to be coherent and detailed, or justice wouldn't be served. Christine would likely give him hell again for pushing, too soon, her fragile young patient. Well so be it. She wasn't always right.

He knew he'd eventually figure out who'd killed the victim, a newborn baby, probably long before he understood what had killed his marriage. He turned the ignition key and nodded to the Eagles Club, hoping he finally had had enough of the place, but pretty sure he'd be back again, same as usual, the next day.

3

ABATHA COX HAD TURNED ELEVEN earlier in the summer, though there was no celebration, nor had there ever been for any other birthday, for the girl lived alone with her grandmother in an old trailer court midway down an Upper Mississippi River bluff. Her parents had abandoned her long ago, so there was no smell of birthday candles melting while father and mother sang out of tune and clapped when she blew out all eleven candles in the cramped trailer sitting not quite level just above the railroad tracks. Her grandmother bought packaged chocolate snack cakes frosted with a curl of tasteless icing. She had candles, but no matches, and she never liked to sing, so Abatha quietly ate both cupcakes in the living room in front of her aquarium. Abatha's new birthday fish, quivering like shiny party favors, hung suspended in their pet store plastic bags slowly acclimating to the aquarium's temperature.

Since the trailer park was close enough to the refinery, what they had smelled instead of melting wax on chocolate was what they always smelled, especially when the wind blew the wrong way, as it did most days: the caustic fumes of the gasoline refinery wafting across the river. Even with the windows closed, the burning odor could still be smelled, though her grandmother declared she didn't ever notice it anymore.

Summer was over now, and Abatha was starting school late a few days, and by now everyone knew why. It was because the last Friday of summer was a perfect summer day that demanded one take notice of everything, particularly if one's name was Abatha Cox. That day, the hot air was unusually dry for August and for once the wind wasn't blowing the wrong way and she could smell

14

the rest of the world's beauty. The river was so low that it slid along, shimmering black and silver like a thick oily snake in the main channel, leaving behind it tangles of smooth driftwood and garbage. Abatha loved wandering by herself and had spent much of the summer traipsing through the woods between the trailer park and the river. All of these circumstances possibly explained why it was that she, Abatha Cox, came across the dead baby.

"ABATHA?"

A smartly dressed woman stood in front of the girl, who was sitting on a bench in front of the middle school's administrative offices.

"I'm Christine Ivory. Your grandmother and I spoke yesterday. She said she told you I'd meet you here."

The woman smiled warmly.

Both Abatha and Christine Ivory were dressed in clothes they hadn't worn before. For Abatha, it was a new pair of jeans and a simple green t-shirt, several sizes too large for her tiny frame. She never wore what most of the girls in school wore —tight layers of form-fitting tanks with spaghetti straps and skinny black jeans, all emblazoned with fashionable, mall-store logos. The fact that only a few of the girls had started to develop curves made it seem even more ludicrous that they displayed themselves in such a racy way. Her grandmother called girls who dressed like that sluts and wouldn't have allowed Abatha to buy slutty clothes, even if she wanted to. That suited Abatha fine. She preferred simple clothes that let her fade into the woodwork.

Christine wore a ribbed, camel-colored designer sweater dress, and shiny black boots. She had bought both items at a consignment shop after she visited her mother in the city the previous weekend.

She had told her mother she had a date and went shopping instead. She would have come up with any excuse to leave her mother's apartment early that day, though she had tried to force herself to stay. Her mother had never gotten over being abandoned by her father, and Christine's presence reminded her of that as yet unhealed wound. The moment she arrived, her mother started picking. When she checked her watch at the consignment store that day, she realized she'd barely managed to last two hours at her mother's.

Christine's hair was swept back elegantly in a simple comb. This week she had colored it a vibrant shade of red with a splash of platinum blond at the nape of her neck. She planned the effect of the red and white and coordinated her entire wardrobe for the next two weeks, down to her hosiery and jewelry. The wardrobe plan was detailed in hangers labeled by the date the outfit would be worn. Christine Ivory didn't care if her obsessive planning made her "borderline" on many of the personality disorder tests she gave her patients. This obsession with clothing organization didn't control her life. Nothing controlled her life.

"I'll be with you these first few days you're back at school. Let's go and talk for a few minutes, then we'll get you settled into your classroom."

Christine Ivory waited while the girl got to her feet. Abatha was a pretty child, too thin, all eyes and bony elbows. Christine Ivory assessed the girl rapidly and quietly, trying to learn as much as she could without having to ask.

Unfortunately the girl's grandmother had been almost useless, so absorbed in her own losses and dramas. Christine had attempted to focus Margaret Cox on Abatha and her needs. But she wanted to talk about being abandoned first by her husband and then by her children. She seemed to have forgotten that her granddaughter had just been traumatized.

Christine had that effect on many people. They immediately opened up to her, revealing losses and heartbreak, which made sense given her chosen profession, but frankly she felt they hoped she'd instantly make everything better, as if she could wipe away years of error and shame as simply as she rolled a lint brush over her fine second-hand wool suits.

Maybe that was why Christine liked scouring the consignment shops for finds. It was both uncomplicated and gratifying to snap up a beautiful and practically unworn designer piece, and then negotiate an even better price. What the secrets and sins of the original owners were didn't matter in the least, though she could easily sense them as she fingered the brocades and cashmeres squashed together on the clothing racks. There were obviously as many hardships and tragedies as there were finely made used silk suits and lightly worn Italian leather jackets for sale, and cheap. That some down-on-her-luck woman had come here to unload an exquisitely tailored hunter-green dress, and it could be hers for just pennies on the dollar, was just not her problem.

Abatha, of course, *was* her problem. And different, she knew the moment she laid eyes on the tiny girl. She had the expression of a shell-shocked war vet. How a child, so young, could empty her face of any clue as to what she was thinking Christine didn't know.

So, for now, she would have to absorb knowledge about this damaged little girl. She mentally reviewed the case notes she'd read before heading to work. The girl's mother had a criminal drug record. Social services had found Abatha, as a toddler, in a broken-down shack near the river. When they discovered her during a drug raid, it was during the heat of summer and Abatha was covered in mosquito bites and had a diaper rash that required intensive care to heal. The child had seen pediatricians up until the previous six months, so the deterioration of her mother's life had been only recent. Her father had escaped the authorities, but left behind his meth lab equipment. Abatha's mother didn't fight when the girl was taken from her. She was too strung out on meth to complain about much of anything.

Christine read the packet full of letters Abatha's mother had sent from the out-of-state detention facility that housed meth addicts. Margaret had kept the letters from Abatha and apparently told the girl her mother was dead. Abatha's mother, Betsey, had written in long, frantic sentences that dipped as they crossed the page, dragged lower and lower by the weight of the writer's sense of guilt, gradually becoming completely illegible, with only words like "sorry" and "forgive" clear near the end of each letter. She obviously tried to make the words more readable, underlining important statements and layering words with multiple colors of inks to try, somehow, to clarify her grief. "I never wanted to hurt you!" she wrote time and again, underlining and circling the "never."

Christine waited, and the girl gathered her things and followed her to the office they'd assigned her, down the hall and around the corner from the middle school's administrative office.

The girl stood in the doorway until Christine coaxed her inside and closed the door.

"Please, sit down."

Abatha sat.

Christine smiled at her again. "I'm here to answer any questions you have and listen to whatever you want to tell me. About anything."

Christine watched the girl's expression. Some children trusted quickly. For others it took time. There were a few who never got there, and Christine feared Abatha might be one of those. It was completely unpredictable when a child might move from one level of trust to the next, and many started off the way Abatha did—keeping a careful distance or just remaining in a state of denial, which might seem like a relief to all concerned.

But denial was not proof of recovery. In fact, it was far from it. Christine knew that, eventually, the memories of the horror would return, and her professional training taught her that these types of memories could suddenly be recalled at the worst time, long after the treatment had ended, and when everyone thought things had returned to normal.

There never really was a normal. No one knew that better than she.

"Do you know whose class you're in this year?"

Abatha's expression remained unchanged. Then, she smiled and spoke. "Mrs. Luther." She added, "You must know that already." She smiled again, but Christine knew it meant nothing. The look in her eyes had not changed.

"Yes," Christine smiled back, "of course I did."

"I'm only here at school because they make me come here." The phrase was defiant but the tone wasn't. Abatha sounded like an ordinary eleven-year-old girl, on the slightly shy side.

"They?"

"She, I meant. My grandmother." Abatha looked away for a moment, and then faced Christine again. The smallest of clarifications had made Abatha uncomfortable, Christine could see that, but the girl rapidly composed her face.

"Even though your grandmother is 'making' you come to school, are there some subjects you like?" Christine leaned forward ever so slightly, closing that distance between herself and Abatha as carefully as she could and in a way she hoped wouldn't frighten her. She leaned one elbow on the arm of her chair, and put her finger thoughtfully on her lip.

She hoped the pose would be convincing. She wasn't sure Abatha would take the bait.

"I'm an A student in everything." Abatha answered with the hint of sing-song in her voice.

"You're a smart girl." Christine leaned forward a touch more. "What subjects do you like the best?"

Christine wondered if Abatha had the energy to keep up what she knew was an act. Unless the girl was so layered by the multiple levels of abuse she'd endured, some in her records some possibly not, then there was going to be a long struggle to get to her core. Christine tried to casually observe her arms for telltale signs of self-mutilation, or any other physical evidence that might signify the level of self-worth the child felt. Nail polish. Cigarette burns. Abatha, if she was a cutter, was careful not to reveal the obvious signs.

Christine could see Abatha was observing her closely. "I like your hair."

"Thank you. I like it, too."

"Does it always look like that?"

Christine let Abatha rest from her questions for a while. Sometimes that was the way in.

"Actually, no. I'm always changing it up."

"Really?"

"Every couple of weeks, actually. Sometimes I go back to a previous shade if it goes with something I plan to wear."

"I asked my grandmother if I could dye my hair. She said no."

"Maybe you'll get your wish when you grow up. I started coloring my hair when I went to college."

Abatha went silent again. She turned away and stared at the wall. Christine waited.

"You know everything about me, don't you?"

"Everything?"

Abatha remained silent.

Christine knew she'd have to be more patient with this one, though sometimes she wished she didn't have to. She realized that she was more often becoming irritated with her patients and how long it took to get through to them. She worried she was getting burned out and wondered if it was starting to show. One of her most recent cases had almost done her in. She had counseled an eight-year-old girl who had watched as their step father repeatedly sodomized her four-year-old brother. She knew she shouldn't think it, but it was merciful the boy died from internal trauma of years of abuse.

Christine knew she couldn't claw her way through that girl's layers of pain, anymore than she could force Abatha to evaluate her recent, and past, experiences until she was ready to talk about them. She thought she'd try anyway.

"What do you think I know about you?" she asked, cautiously.

Without moving muscle, Abatha shrank back into herself. The school bell rang, and Abatha got up without as much as a sigh.

"I'll see you tomorrow, Abatha."

Christine closed the door and sat in her chair, her head in her hands. Her Blackberry had been buzzing urgently deep inside the hip pocket of her sweater dress the entire time she'd been with Abatha. And she knew very well who was trying to get in contact with her. It was the county.

She inhaled and checked in with the office secretary. She was told that the detective Arvo Thorson was on his way to see her. He'd be arriving within the hour. This meant a week that had starting off badly was only going to go downhill.

Arvo had all of the qualities that made Christine Ivory want to go home and reorganize her closet. Back when they both had been together in high school years earlier, he had been the handsome blond captain of the football team. His high school girlfriend was the prom queen, Helen Cotner. In short, his life had that storybook quality that hers would always lack.

Christine had been the "smart girl" though no one knew she'd been valedictorian—in those days, achievements like sports championships and having a hot car or a hot body were the only accomplishments recognized. Certainly not scholarship. She wished she could have skipped most of her junior and senior year, it was such a waste of time, but there wasn't an option to test out and graduate early. She kept to herself, had few friends, hung out with the losers and weirdos for a while, then no one at all. She did nothing to make herself attractive in those days. Her long hair hung down over her face, and she hid her figure in shapeless, men's work shirts and baggy painter's pants. No one ever came close enough to notice the clear spark of intelligence in her eyes, her porcelain, blemish-free skin, her delicately curved lips and carefully painted fingernails.

Helen had every boy after her, and that was widely known by everyone except Arvo. She'd taken every opportunity to cheat on him. Christine didn't take pity on him back then and she still didn't. He and the prom queen divorced in the past year. The gossip was that he'd been drinking again. And of course he'd put on some weight since high school. She had to admit that some might still consider the man good looking in a rugged, worn-out sort of way. Close up, the hollow gray expression, unshaven face, watery eyes, and slight paunch told that he was years past his attractive days.

So she'd ignored the ringing phone when she saw it was him calling. She had, of course, professional reasons for putting him off. But she also enjoyed the thought of his squirming and didn't care that it was wrong. So she dawdled longer by making a few notes about the day's session with Abatha and thought about her approach for the next day. The girl's face wasn't yet tattooed in her brain like the rest of her patients' faces, but she knew it was coming and dreaded it. Maybe she should take that sabbatical the department head kept suggesting. Or maybe she should restart therapy. She should know better by now that no one was ever really "cured." You just ended up with healthier coping strategies.

Schadenfreude, that delightful German word that meant the joy of watching another's pain, was not a healthy coping mechanism. Still the thought of seeing Arvo, who she knew was still completely depressed about his wife, gave her a smug, though somewhat uneasy, pleasure. Pleasure, even the bad kind, was getting harder to come by these days.

Christine checked her Blackberry to refresh her mind on the day's schedule. Thorson had not, of course, scheduled time with her electronically and that annoyed her. She declined the weekly department meeting and reluctantly put time on her calendar for him. She stood up and looked into her bag for her make-up kit. She noticed that the shade of lipstick she wore wasn't exactly working with her look, so she scrubbed it off and applied a deeper color.

She repacked her bag and headed back to the office. She hoped Thorson would be on time. She hated when people messed with her schedule. Most of all, she despised people who had everything going for them and still managed to have the time and energy to screw up everyone's lives, including their own. She smoothed down her dress, recalling the day she picked it up, lightly sensing again some unknown former wearer's troubles, and oddly irritated by the interruption to her thoughts. She worked to focus her irritation on Arvo instead. She knew some of her ire might be misplaced, but there were not enough people in the world to be blamed for the horrors she'd seen. Everyone was responsible. Even people like Thorson.

4

THE COUNTY BUILDING ROSE like a citadel from the river bluff at the intersection of three markedly different landscapes. North and east of the building, the land fell down to where the clear blue waters of the St. Croix River dumped into dirty brown Mississippi River. Eagles soared overhead and speed boats darted around the heavy barge traffic.

West of the building, the land unfolded itself to form the northern boundary of the Great Plains. A patchwork of corn fields and pastures was stitched together with blacktopped county roads and gravel tractor paths and accented by the occasional meandering creek.

To the south lay the driftless area, a corner of the state left untouched in the last glacial era, ending some 15,000 years earlier. The deeply carved and thickly wooded river valleys formed a back country less arable than the fertile plain to the west.

At this crossroads of contrasting landscapes, another discordant assembly was about to take place. Arvo Thorson arrived for his meeting with Christine Ivory by nearly crashing his Ford Taurus into her Volkswagen Passat as they both raced for the same primo parking spot.

She kept herself from giving the rude driver the finger until she knew exactly who it was, and then went ahead. He nodded and allowed her to claim the spot. They met up again at the metal detectors.

"Christine, it's so good to see you again," he said as he held out his badge and his sidearm for the guard's inspection.

"The sarcasm has gotten boring, Thorson. It's been boring for years." She tossed her keys and Blackberry into the tray and briskly walked through the detector, reclaiming her items once cleared through. She headed off and Thorson caught up with her at the elevators. He pressed her floor number gallantly.

Thorson felt his mood lift while Christine's dropped. When they arrived at her office, he was ready to usher her inside with a gentlemanly flourish when she cut him off.

"It's not 10 yet. Give me a few moments."

"No problem," he said, finding a hard bench in the hallway outside. He checked his analog watch and saw he had 15 minutes to kill, so he headed to the bathroom. He stood for longer than necessary at the urinal, lost in thought about how next he could torment his coworker. Then he checked his reflection in the mirror, jauntily winked at himself, and strode back to Christine's office.

A secretary appeared in the hallway and informed him that Christine Ivory was ready to see him. Inside, he removed his jacket and tossed it in a side chair where it lay rumpled. He knew this would bother Christine, she hated a mess. She got up and hung it on a hanger behind her door.

Thorson made a show out of rolling up his sleeves, clearing his nasal cavities with a loud sniff, and tucking in his shirt. He sat down and created the widest stance he could think of.

Christine walked to her side of the desk, sat down in her enormous and expensive-looking calf leather desk chair (a find she snapped up at an estate sale), opened up her notepad, lined up her Blackberry precisely one inch from the side of her notepad, and laid down three freshly sharpened pencils as if they were hash marks ready to score the game they both knew they were playing with each other.

Christine waited for Thorson to speak. This was always the important part of their interaction. She refused to say anything first, thinking it the sign of weakness. Thorson knew this and granted it, the only accommodation he would make for her.

"Where do things stand with the girl?" he asked after a suitable time.

Christine appraised him. She knew his irritation with her brought needed color into his ash-pale face. His ice blue eyes were alert, almost captivating, but as for the rest of him ... he was growing more paunchy and stained by the day. For a moment she almost felt sorry for him.

She was ready to answer that the girl was not ready yet, but her secretary Sharon rapped on the door and interrupted.

"Yes," Christine asked, aware that she sounded irritated. It was important to her to retain control. She inhaled deeply, as she had learned in her Yoga class, and then exhaled slowly.

"It's someone from Senator Jane Columbus-Power's office. The senator wants to have a word with you."

A senator calling to speak to her. Directly. "What would Senator Jane Columbus-Powers want from me?" Christine knew it wasn't necessary to say the whole name again, but she wanted Thorson to know of this little victory.

"She's called several times this morning and I told her you weren't in yet. Do you want me to take a message?" Christine knew it aggravated Sharon to put anything off, she didn't really care to appease an important senator like Jane Columbus-Powers. Sharon just wanted to end her day with a clean desk.

"I apologize, Arvo, I will need to take this call."

Thorson smirked. "I guess I'll wait. As usual."

"Put her through," Christine said. She could see that made Sharon happy. Christine hit the speaker phone button and after that, Sharon announced the senator's name again.

"Ms. Ivory, it's Senator Columbus-Powers. I apologize for interrupting your day." The senator's voice was strong, purposeful. She needed every ounce of that its strength for the reelection battle she was waging. Everyone in the country knew that. A conservative with a family values agenda, the senator's message played especially well in the mostly rural county. A few years younger than Arvo and Christine, she shared their hometown but not their politics.

Her opponent's liberal, working-person's agenda was making his standing rise in the polls. It helped his cause tremendously that the economy was tanking and everyone associated with the incumbent president's agenda was feeling the pain.

None of this was lost on Christine. A powerful senator needed something from her and Arvo Thorson was there to witness it. Finally things were looking up.

"Senator what can I do for you today? I am in the middle of a meeting with Detective Arvo Thorson but certainly can take a moment for you." Christine was pleased her voice had the correct level of bossiness in it.

"I was just talking to the county sheriff. Bill Ruud is a good friend of mine. He speaks very highly of you and says you're the best social worker in the county."

Christine was fairly certain that the county sheriff couldn't have picked her out of a line up.

"This terrible tragedy about the baby and the little girl that found it. What an awful, awful discovery." The senator's voice was cool and silky with empathetic tones.

Christine inspected her nails to keep from rolling her eyes at Thorson. She knew the senator wasn't calling to get personally involved in her line of work. Still, she had to play along as best she could. To do so meant she needed to keep her focus on the voice on the phone, and try to avoid sneaking looks at Thorson to catch his reaction.

"Our office has learned the girl lives in troubling circumstances." Not difficult to learn this, the family's story had been splashed all over the newspapers. "Father missing, mother incarcerated due to meth abuse, lives with her grandmother." The senator masterfully maintained an appropriately subdued tone of shock in her voice.

Thorson coughed, startling Christine. She shot him a hostile look for distracting her from her moment of triumph. "Senator, we see these kinds of cases all the time." She spoke quickly and knew she sounded impatient.

"It's shocking how the lack of strong moral family values in parts of the county can affect our children."

Now Christine had to say something. "I happen to believe that economics impacts family situations more than morals. Professional ethics prevent me from giving you specific examples that I see every day, Senator, or this phone call would go on even longer than it has."

The senator was on the defensive. "I truly apologize for taking up your valuable time. As I mentioned, when I spoke with the sheriff, he emphasized the importance of what you do and how well you do it. Bill and I had a heart-to-heart about the tough circumstances of some people living in the county and he praised you – in fact he said he doesn't know how the department could ever be thankful enough for your efforts."

Now Christine couldn't avoid rolling her eyes. She caught herself as soon as she saw Thorson stifling a laugh into another cough. She put the phone on mute as the senator went on.

"Would you mind!" She snapped.

"I can't help it. The bullshit is being laid on so thick they can smell the stink down the hall."

"Please. Control yourself." She snapped the speaker back on as the senator was concluding all of her remarks about the 'little people like Christine who so tremendously contribute.'

"I'll try not to take up much more of your time. The reason I'm calling is that my office wants to help in some way in easing this family's burden."

"No one is stopping you, Senator. I would think that given your office, there is much you can do that might help a lot of the burdens many families face." Christine made her politics clear.

"Yes, Ms. Ivory. Our office works day and night with initiatives supportive of the family values that are so important in keeping our communities strong." The voice was still powerful, road-tested from the rigors of the season's hard fought campaign.

"Senator I'm sure you're doing everything possible to support your agenda. Not much of it trickles down into the lives of the people I see. Again, professional ethics prevents me from giving you much in the way of specifics."

Christine paused knowing she had the floor. "What exactly do you want from me today, I have kept Detective Thorson waiting long enough."

"Thank you for being so considerate of my time, Ms. Ivory," Thorson broke in at last.

"Yes, I apologize to the detective." This time the senator's apology didn't include any kind words from the sheriff, though he would have obviously been more acquainted with Thorson's skills and abilities than with Christine's.

"As I mentioned, my office is interested in trying to help this poor girl. We are wondering what might be a good time for her to receive support from our office. The sheriff told me that only you were in a position to judge whether the girl might be fit for a small presentation, perhaps at her school. As a way of helping both her, and the community, heal from this terrible tragedy."

Christine's face reddened. She glanced at Thorson. She could see that his face had hardened as well.

"Senator," Christine began, struggling to control the edge to her voice. "This office will not be involved in providing any public information whatsoever as to the status of a patient, particularly a child. I don't know what the sheriff may have told you, but, it will be a cold day in – "

" – I'm sorry to interrupt," Thorson said jerking the speaker phone in his direction. "What Ms. Ivory is trying to say is that we can't release any information that might threaten the investigation."

"Of course, detective, my office understands the importance of maintaining careful control of the ongoing investigation. Our goal, and I apologize to Ms. Ivory if I misspoke, our single aim with the poor girl is to show that the community is behind her." Christine slammed the mute on. "Don't you dare speak over me, Arvo. I'm telling you. This is a bunch of crap about their agenda and I'll be damned if they are going to use me, or my patient, to increase their poll numbers."

"Christine, you need to calm down. We all know what's going on. You don't need to be rude."

"Do NOT ever tell me to calm down. I'm warning you, Arvo." Christine unmuted the speaker. "It's very simple, senator." She had managed to get a grip on herself, at least slightly. "I'll be brief. I will not be involved in granting you the permission to trot this girl out onto your platform. In fact, I will do everything in my power to keep 'your office' and the girl, as far apart as possible. Good day."

Christine hung up. She let go of her fury. "I do not play any-one's political games, not with a powerful senator and not in this office. This is completely ridiculous that they would stoop to this level, a poor girl like Abatha who did nothing but stumble out from her own tragic life and right into someone else's. I can't even begin to describe my outrage."

"A moron could see that. A moron could see a lot, looking at you." Thorson gave Christine the once-over with his eyes. "I should inform you that unlike most women, anger does not make you pretty."

Christine ignored his lame attempt at mocking her. "Doesn't this bother you at all?"

"Of course it does. Look, anyone paying even the slightest at-tention to the campaign knows that the senator has been using Somerset Hills, her home town, as some kind of great example of every town USA moral values. That mega church her father leads shows up in every political ad and speech she's been making for the past year. So think about it Christine, if you can for a moment put your rage aside."

She knew he meant, "Calm the hell down."

"Here is a baby being thrown away in her own backyard. Doesn't say much about her hometown family values, now does it?"

"Arvo, I do not have the time or energy to interpret what the senator's motives might be in an attempt to pacify my temper. How dare anyone call me and make the kind of request she's making. Particularly some hell-bent far right candidate who says she puts families first."

Christine threw herself back into her chair, spun around and got up. She walked to the wide floor-to-ceiling windows flanking one of her walls and furiously cranked the blinds open. Still morning, the sunlight streamed in through her east-facing windows. From her sixth floor office, she could see all the way to the river and a few miles beyond to where the neighboring state bordered. Barges jammed the river, winter was coming and there was much grain to be hauled downriver and much coal to be hauled upriver over the few short months before winter would take hold.

Christine looked upriver in the direction of the refinery, to where she knew Abatha had found the baby on a deserted stretch of shoreline. Who knew what visions were in the girl's head. She might be the only person who would ever hear them, and only if she could manage to get Abatha to tell her.

Finally, when she had calmed enough, she turned around and only remembered Thorson's presence when she saw him sitting quietly waiting for her. A calm expression was on his face. He too had been thinking about something.

She sat down and smoothed the wrinkles out of her dress.

"So. What is it you've wanted to see me about?"

"I think you know why I'm here. We always end up together on these kinds of cases."

"Just be specific. Please?" Christine had grown weary and it wasn't even noon yet.

"The girl. You know I need to have a chance to talk to her."

"Yes. I know." Christine turned to the window again. The strong light made a heavy spotlight on her face. She didn't squint, in fact, it relaxed her to have something so pure and light touching her, especially after that call.

"When do you think she might be ready? You know I need to get to her as soon as I can, before the memories start fading. Or she starts wondering whether she dreamed the whole thing up."

"She's hardly said a word to me, but I have a feeling that this girl's memory is going to stay sharp. Give me a few more days, Arvo."

"How about tomorrow?"

"Arvo? Please. She needs more time. Two days. With the option of putting you off longer if my assessment changes."

"I'll call you tomorrow, Christine."

Thorson got up and straightened his shirt again. Christine saw the gun hanging under his left arm and that reminded her she had something of his. She got up from her desk and retrieved his coat, neatly hung on her hanger behind the door.

"The day after tomorrow is the soonest I want to hear from you," she said, holding the jacket in front of him.

He took his jacket and headed to her door. "Tomorrow."

5

ARVO THORSON ARRIVED in his basement office and tossed his coat in the direction of a chair. It missed and landed on the floor. Thorson left it there.

His cell phone buzzed again. It had been buzzing steadily throughout his meeting with Christine and even though he knew who it was, he avoided answering. Before he threw himself into his desk chair, he dug the phone out of his pocket.

The display flashed six new messages, listing each caller.

6) Helen

5) Helen

4) Helen

3) Helen

2) Helen

1) Helen

Playing Russian roulette, Thorson took his chances and arrowed down to message number four, sent about an hour earlier.

"No check. On my way."

He glanced at his watch, forgetting again that his phone had a clock. The calculation put Helen's arrival in the next ten minutes. He presumed messages five and six clarified her timing.

Thorson grabbed his coat and was about to head out the back when Juney Janette called to him in her kewpie doll voice.

"Arvo, I gotta talk to you about something."

He opened the emergency exit door and urged her to hurry out with him.

"Where are you going? You just got here!"

Thorson slammed the door in time to see Helen making her way in. Janette saw her too.

"You're late with the check again, aren't you?"

"Nobody knows me like you, Juney girl."

Arvo hustled Juney outside to a spot around the corner and out of the sight from the basement windows.

"So what do you have for me?"

"Damn you, Thorson. We're out, and I didn't grab my cigarettes."

"Sorry, but you know you really should cut down."

Thorson towered over Juney, but the tiny woman made up for it with her ample girth and sheer determination. She gave Thorson a scowl.

"I know, I know. Your grandmother smoked until she was one hundred and only quit because she started to fall asleep with a lit cigarette in her mouth. And that's your excuse." Thorson made a face back at her.

"So would you shut up about it? I haven't had my morning smoke yet, and now you got me out here."

"You're the one who wanted to talk to me."

***

PEOPLE WHO CAME TO KNOW Juney over the phone made the mistake of not taking her seriously. At first. The criminal investigation department's clerk was not to be trifled with, particularly when it came to her meticulously maintained files. Juney had worked for the department since she was nineteen, which meant thirty years of filing. In addition to cataloging and filing the various criminal case records, Juney had another entire carefully organized encyclopedia in her head.

Retrieving the paper file was rarely necessary as Juney could spit out the minutest detail, even from cases decades earlier, and all in a moment's notice.

"That new case, the John Doe baby."

"What about it? I haven't even had a chance to talk to the girl yet." Thorson looked up six floors. He knew he was standing directly below Christine's window. He took a few steps out into the sunlight, positioning himself directly in her line of sight.

"Oh, I forgot. I brought you a present." Thorson handed her the pack of cigarettes he'd been carrying around in his jacket pocket since summer. He'd quit then after an episode of chest pain convinced him he was about to have a heart attack. He realized that the worst part of his life was behind him, but that surviving Helen in her new role, as his ex-wife, wasn't going to be much easier. The cigarettes would have to go.

Juney lit up and leaned against the building. Thorson waited patiently. He knew she hadn't forgotten she had something to tell him. He glanced up again and thought he saw movement in Christine's window.

"This isn't the first time a dead baby has washed up in that particular area of the river, you know," Juney said, taking another long drag off her cigarette. "Now this goes back before your time."

"You go back before everyone's time, Juney."

"Are you making a crack about my age? I'm not THAT much older than you. You know, you aren't looking that good, Arvo. You need to lose some weight. And that's saying a lot, coming from me."

Thorson bowed his head slightly. "You got me."

She took another drag. "May I continue now?"

"You have the floor, madam."

"It was 1987. The Twins got their first championship that year if you recall."

"Yes, I recall. I was graduating from college that year. Just by the seat of my pants—I was on the five-year plan. The Twins celebration was just another day drinking on campus at the U. Had plans to get married the next summer. One big fairytale life back in those days."

"Not much of a fairytale for one baby. The day after the big World Series championship celebration, they found it. Almost exactly the same place as this one the girl found last Saturday."

"And?"

"Cold case. Near as they could tell, the baby was born alive, then tossed in the river. A girl. Lots of women were tested at the time, but no one was identified as a possible relation. Near as they could tell, the baby had been in the water for a few months."

"Any word on results from this one?"

Juney exhaled and sent a puff of smoke out her nose. "Nothing yet, it will be awhile."

Thorson waited again. He knew Juney. Beyond her encyclopedic memory of the facts, she had a gift for making connections that could not be derived from the available facts. Thorson called it "the hunch factor."

"What's the hunch factor? I know you have one."

She had been waiting for him to ask. "I even looked up the records on that old case this time. You know me, I don't need to have the paper. But something is making the hair go up on the back of my neck. Even I know this one is way, way beyond even the hunch factor."

"What is it?"

Juney lit up a second cigarette.

"Even though these two deaths are twenty years apart, I don't think it's just a coincidence that they ended up on the same stretch of shoreline. I just know there's a connection here, Arvo. A really strong one."

"Twenty years, Juney." He whistled. "That's a long time. I bet almost no one even remembers that old case, except you."

"Well, maybe I'm getting a little ding-y in my old age, me going back before everyone's time and all. Did you hear there might be layoffs in the department?"

"Nothing is going to happen to you, Juney, trust me. They'll kick my sorry old ass out of here before anyone else's head hits the chopping block."

Juney snorted. "You? No way. Not with all those commendations you have."

"You've forgotten the lengthy list of disciplinary notices."

"School kid stuff, Arvo. So you've been tardy a couple of times on your paperwork. Maybe don't follow a department protocol to the letter. So what." Juney watched the curl of smoke come off the lighted end of her cigarette. "Anyone can find a replacement clerk."

Arvo patted Juney on the shoulder. He knew she lived alone. Her husband had died in a car accident early in their marriage and that left Juney on her own to raise their two kids. Now that they'd both grown up, she was alone again.

"Trust me. Even if they were stupid enough to try kicking you out of here, they'd have me to deal with. And you know I have a problem with authority."

Juney smiled and finished her second cigarette.

"So that's what you have for me today?" Thorson asked.

"That's it for now. I'll keep you informed."

"You do that."

"And by the way, tell your ex-wife to stop calling me looking for you."

Yes, Arvo had felt his phone buzzing non-stop. "She knows you, like the rest of us do. You know where everything is, Juney."

"Maybe if you'd answer your phone and keep on time, she'd get off my back."

"You've made your point." Arvo opened the emergency exit door and let Juney back inside.

She gave him one last look. "I'll tell her I haven't seen you today and don't know when you'll be in."

"That's my girl," Arvo laughed.

After Juney left, Arvo retrieved the nagging phone from his pocket and scrolled through his message list again. He deleted every text from Helen and shut the phone off, shoving it back in his pocket. Then he walked out from the building until he was standing at the edge of the summit. A few more steps and the land started sloping down to the river valley. He turned and took another look up the side of the building, squinting in the reflections that shot off from the glass.

Christine came to the window again and looked down, seeing him. She watched without moving. He waved at her and she turned away sharply. He laughed, then got his phone out of his pocket again and stared at it.

"Helen, you are a complete pain in the ass," he told his phone, before turning it on and dialing her number.

She answered and released a stream of abuse into his ear.

"Where do you want to meet?" he squeezed in, at last. She named a place, told him not to be late, and threatened him with some as yet undetermined punishment if he was.

He hung up, called Juney, and learned that it was true that Helen had left the office. He took one last glance up to the sixth floor, then headed inside to his office, and some overdue paperwork Juney had left for him.

6

ARVO THORSON GOT LOST on the way to Drifters. It shouldn't have been that difficult, he'd been there many times before. Hop onto Highway 61, cross the Mississippi, you're there.

Unfortunately road construction was going on, and the only route to Drifters was no longer a ten-minute drive. Thorson knew that, and had he planned ahead, he could have adjusted accordingly. Thorson rarely planned ahead.

By the time he arrived at the riverside bar, it was after one and Helen had been waiting for over an hour. He walked to her table and noticed a man slipping away just as he appeared.

"About damn time!" his wife said.

"It's good to see you, too, Helen," he answered. "Can I buy you a drink?"

Helen's eyes answered for her.

Thorson sat down. Helen was still gorgeous, even in her early forties. A tiny, curvy, blond, with a smile accented by two dimples (though Thorson had rarely seen her smile) she thought herself overweight and had constantly dieted, no matter how often Thorson told her she was beautiful. Her creamy complexion was velvety smooth. Had she lived on one of the coasts, she'd have easily picked up modeling jobs. She looked years younger than he did. Thorson still felt jealous when he saw men in the bar sneaking looks at her. Despite everything, even the sight of her cheating on him, he still wanted her back.

Even when she opened her mouth to curse him, Thorson couldn't help feeling a passion for her beautiful teeth. He'd remembered the feeling of running his tongue along them. He knew he was a complete asshole for loving her, as Juney had so often reminded him. He wished he knew how to get rid of the useless feelings he had for her.

A waitress stopped by and took Thorson's order. An appletini for Helen, a whiskey sour for him. He knew he shouldn't be drinking during working hours. He knew a lot of things that he paid no heed to.

Their table near the window opened out onto a view of the pretty marina lined with pleasure boats. For a weekday, the place was already busy with boats coming and going, but at this time of the year in Minnesota, if the weather was good, people got into their boats no matter what day it was. A mild breeze blew through the open windows.

"So how have you been, Helen?" he asked, almost forgetting that they were adversaries.

"Arvo, can we cut the crap?"

The waitress returned with their drinks, annoying Helen into a scowl when she momentarily forgot who had ordered what and had to ask.

Helen took hers and set it in front of her. Thorson knew she wouldn't drink any of it, too fattening. She took the swizzle stick out and picked at the table with it.

Arvo gulped down a few swallows of his drink then cleared his throat. "Helen, you know I didn't want any of this. I know that legally our marriage is over and has been so for three months now."

"Officially," Helen interrupted.

"Helen, I really think we could start over. It's not too late."

Helen laughed haughtily at him, shaking her head. Arvo noticed a man at the bar watching them closely. The man wore a pricey sports jacket over his bulging belly, and everything about him seemed overdone. Arvo could smell the heavy scent of his expensive cologne even from twenty feet away. It was as if the stuff clung to everything in the room. Even Helen, only a few feet away, seemed to reek of it.

Arvo smiled uncomfortably and nodded at the guy.

Helen noticed and snapped, "What's wrong with you?" She gouged the table with her swizzle stick, and Arvo noticed the perfect, blood-red nail polish on her perfectly sculpted nails.

"When are you going to get it? Don't you see enough nutty relationships in your line of work? People together who shouldn't be together, some who end up killing each other?"

Helen noticed her voice was getting too much attention from the other patrons. She moved her chair closer to the table. "Did you go to that therapist they told you to go see?"

"The nervous guy with the sweaty hands? By the way he's just getting divorced. Again."

Helen didn't bat an eye. "Clearly you haven't actually been to see him."

"I don't plan on going, ever."

"As I see it, your problem is you don't like to lose. You don't like to be wrong. This has nothing to do with our relationship."

"Helen, thank you for your analysis, but I don't need it." Thorson drained the rest of his drink and felt the pleasant tingling sensation in the backs of his legs. He motioned to the waitress to bring him another. "I don't have a problem, other than being in love with my wife."

"Ex-wife."

"On paper only."

"You are totally out of your mind, Arvo." Helen leaned back and tossed her hair. She glanced again at the man sitting at the bar. He nodded slightly. She looked back at Arvo and took a deep breath. Arvo could see her taking a moment to reconsider. Maybe he'd gotten through to her, this time.

"I want you to stop this. I've been patient with you, and despite what you may think, I have tried hard not to hurt you. When I gave up on that approach, I decided it might be better to hurt you, because you're just not getting it, even though we're divorced. You don't quit, ever."

Thorson's second drink arrived, and he began to drain that one. He still thought there was an outside chance, a very small one, that this was the time he would turn her around.

"I'm going to be perfectly clear with you," Helen said with the hint of a smile. The two dimples came out and for a moment. Thorson lost himself in his alcohol-buzzed admiration of them.

"Are you listening to me? Look at me, Arvo."

He looked at her, his beautiful wife.

"I don't want you. I don't love you. I haven't loved you ever, not even when you were the king and I was the queen."

His beautiful ex-wife.

"I just wanted to be the queen and you happened to be the king of everything, back then."

The flaming color blossomed on her gorgeous cheeks. Arvo remembered kissing them and the soft feel of her skin on his lips. He knew everything about his love for her was wrong, but even just breathing next to her filled him with ecstasy, as stupid as it sounded even to him. He remembered feeling a sort of kinship with a man who'd just been beaten nearly to death by his wife. As they carried him off on a stretcher, bloodied and nearly unconscious, he said to the EMTs, "God I love that bitch."

"Please, Arvo, stop tormenting me. Can we set up the automatic transfer for the alimony, please?"

Arvo didn't answer. He opened his wallet and handed her the envelope addressed to her containing the check he should have sent weeks ago. That was the cue for the man sitting at the bar.

He walked over and escorted Helen out and down to one of the big expensive boats in the marina. With gas prices the way they were, and this man able to command a craft that size, Arvo wondered why Helen needed his money at all. Arvo watched them board it and motor away, Helen's sunlit blond hair blowing like a silky flag in the wind.

The waitress left him the tab and Arvo paid up. Leaving the bar, he knew he'd need to sober up before he went anywhere.

Despite the handicap of a couple of whiskey sours and the acrid aftertaste of his battle with Helen, he remembered he was close to where the little girl had discovered the baby's body. He checked the notes in his car and grabbed his jacket.

The spot was downriver about a mile or so from Drifters. The baby had been found directly across the river from the gasoline refinery. Not too hard to miss, the gasoline refinery towered across the river and reminded him of an Escher woodcut: all interconnected tubes and stacks organized like a crazy mirrored maze in a funhouse. The bar he'd just left had been carefully constructed so that the view looked away from the refinery. At least the refinery owners had managed, over the years and out of necessity, to run a little cleaner. He noticed that the air at least smelled fresh, which was very different from how it had been in the days when he was growing up just over the hill.

He made his way along the gravel road that fronted the river, surprised to see a few ramshackle trailer homes tucked in the scrubby woods. Anything less movable had been flooded, time and again, over the years. He knew enough of the girl's history to know she spent her early years in one of these places.

He approached a part of the road that had seen lots of tire treads over the past week. Not only had various law enforcement departments made regular trips to the location, but all of the major news outlets from the Cities had done pieces here. Horror sells on the six o'clock news.

Ahead he saw a few remnants of the crime scene tape marking the general area. He knew he should have already been to this site, particularly when the sheriff called him only minutes after the discovery. Somehow Arvo hadn't made it until now. But this was always how he worked.

He still had twenty yards of thick brush to make his way through to get to the river. All the traffic that had come through made that task a little easier, but not much. Preserving the crime scene was important, but it was likely the infant hadn't been dumped in this location. It was only found here.

Still, he wondered why an eleven-year-old girl would be wandering alone in the desolate, rotted area.

He got to the river and stood on the muddy shore. The stink of the river, this late in the year, was at its peak, and he wondered how long he'd be able to stand the smell. Not too far out from shore, the current was strong and fast and the channel deep. Closer to shore he saw where a tangle of driftwood, dead carp and garbage collected in a pool of backwater.

The girl had spotted the baby there. He'd seen a lot of awful things in his years of detective work. He'd seen people killed in a staggering and endless number of creative and vicious ways. In some cases, the victims had ample warning about exactly how their death would come and who would deliver it to them.

Maybe that was why Helen's bad behavior hadn't really dimmed his love for her. He'd gotten used seeing people treating their nearest and dearest horribly and absolutely nothing changing. Wives returned to their abusive husbands; husbands returned to their abusive wives; guys returned for another friendly game of cards with some cheating son of a bitch. When there was a loaded gun handy, well, accidents sometimes happened. No one ever meant to kill anyone. That's what everyone always said.

And it was often difficult for the most horribly abused victims to agree to put the cruelest of the bastards away. The fact of the matter was that the bad things people did to each other never altered the sick foundation of human relationships, at least the ones he was familiar with. If you loved someone, you loved them, even when they were beating the crap out of you.

Despite that thick skin he'd developed witnessing the inhumanity he'd encountered professionally and personally, he was rapidly feeling sick. He fell to his knees in the stinking river mud and vomited up the two or three whisky sours he'd consumed. And when there wasn't anything left in his stomach to vomit up, he kept retching the sick emptiness.

When it was finally over, his head stopped pounding and he staggered to his feet, sweaty from the sickness that seemed like it would never stop coming out of him. Maybe Helen was right about something being wrong with him. He turned away from the river, got back on the road, and found himself agreeing fully with her assessment, knowing it would do nothing to change how things were.

7

CHRISTINE IVORY WAITED FOR ABATHA Cox in the dump of an office they'd assigned her at Somerset Hills Middle School. She glanced at her Blackberry, noted the time, and saw she was an hour early, which was not a surprise to her as she was compulsively prompt. Her over-preparedness was another symptom, she knew, of neurotic behavior. Arriving early, she ended up circling, either the block around an event she was attending or swirling in thoughts around a much examined issue. Christine hated that she over-thought every aspect of her life, though not out of a fear that her fussiness might be off-putting to others. It was simply emotionally exhausting most of her waking hours, and carried through into her sleeping hours. She habitually dreamt about high school or college, fretting over a lost school schedule, a forgotten locker combination, or her late arrival to class. That none of these fears had ever came to pass in real life— her school days were long behind her—it never diminished the level of anxiety she dreamt each night.

She examined her cuticles and removed a loose hair from the tailored gray jacket she'd snapped up a few weeks ago. She inspected her makeup and hair in her compact, and reevaluated the small adjustment she'd made to her hair color the night before, when she'd added a few platinum highlights to frame her face. She was always adjusting everything, never sure whether it was because it wasn't perfect enough or because she just grew bored that quickly.

She knew she needed more to occupy her evenings. Reading over her casework notes, coloring her hair, and organizing her wardrobe couldn't be considered relaxing hobbies. Intellectually she knew what she needed was a solid relationship with someone, but getting a pet was out of the question. She didn't even want so much as a plant to water. A man? Men were messier than dogs and needier than her worst patients. Her mother should have given up years ago asking about her dating life. Christine always gave the same answer. She was too busy with her career and honestly didn't miss them. Her mother lived alone too, having been divorced since Christine, her only child, was a girl, so Christine had grown used to not having men around her.

The unsightly mess in the room was making her edgy. After meeting with Abatha earlier in the week, she'd requested that the room get some housekeeping attention, but the expression on the school secretary's face told her it wouldn't be happening. She asked whether another, more "professional" location was available, and the secretary went back to updating the principal's calendar without even acknowledging the question.

So, in addition to her briefcase, her Blackberry, and the extra platinum highlights in her hair, Christine brought with her a small box of cleaning supplies. She evaluated the room to narrow in a starting point and determined that today's task would be to clean off the overflowing credenza top. She knew she had no right to do anything other than meet with the girl and provide the level of therapy required, but she would never survive the assignment in this disaster of a room. Used coffee cups, crusted with a mold soufflé, torn public service posters warning children how to avoid various evils and who to contact when they didn't, unused coloring papers, and just plain refuse sat gathering dust and who knew what else.

Christine carried the cups down the hall to the teacher's lounge and dumped the sludgy mess into the sink. She returned and tackled the rest of the mess on top of credenza and noticed that a couple of random scraps had fallen behind it. She was on her hands and knees when she heard the sound of someone clearing his throat behind her.

"That looks good on you," he said.

She snapped to her feet and whipped industrial blue rubber gloves off her hands.

"I wasn't talking about the gloves," Arvo added.

"You're prowling around earlier than usual," she said. "What brings you here, a day before I told you to contact me?"

"I believe what you told me applied to calling you. You should know me better by now. I never call." He couldn't help adding another smart remark. "Just like the rest of the men in your life."

Christine answered plainly. "I won't bother telling you that your sense of humor hasn't ever seemed very funny to me."

"I wasn't joking."

She gave the impression of ignoring him by turning her attention to a stack of water-stained papers, and he gave the impression that he didn't buy it by casually flipping through the case folder on the desk. "Ms. Ivory, I am here on a professional matter. You know that the department occasionally requires that we speak to each other. In my judgment, you owe me a conversation about where the girl stands."

"And I told you to give me another day."

He threw himself into the side chair and rubbed his face in his palms. He knew she could see he was hung over. He also knew that was not news to her.

"Christine, do we need to go through this every time we work together?"

She frowned at him as if to say she wasn't the problem.

"Come on. You know how difficult it is to get the facts when they're still fresh. It's worse with kids. They'll tell you something they are 100 percent sure about and then you find out later that everything they told you was spoon-fed to them by someone else. Then I'll have spent days on some awful case like this and come away with nothing."

Christine put the cleaning supplies away and sat on the edge of her desk.

"Please. I'm asking you. I know you're trying to protect your patient. But, God damn it, Christine, have you forgotten what happened here? Someone threw away a baby, just tossed the poor thing into the river."

He could see she was at least listening. For once. That was a first. "That baby is the child you need to be thinking about. The girl, she's still alive. She's got that going for her."

Christine shifted on the desk and upset a stack of papers uncomfortably wedged underneath her, spilling a folder onto the floor in a cascade of paper. She stooped to attempt to gather them again, then gave up. "The lighting in here is worse than that hole they call your office." She got up and struggled to open the dusty, bent blinds covering a wide window.

"Nothing in this place works!" she said yanking the cord to no avail.

"Here," Arvo said behind her. "Let me see what the problem is."

"Go ahead," she said, folding her arms to make the challenge clear.

"Even when you back down, you don't give up, do you?" He examined the blinds, yanking the cords a couple of times. "Okay, let's try the Zen approach."

"So you're a Buddhist *and* a jerk."

His eyes snapped on her face. "All I'm saying is that forcing things only breaks them. You have to stand back and take a closer look at the machinery sometimes." His eyes traveled up the cords to where they entered the housing.

"See? It's jammed." He located one of the broken pencils she'd tossed in the trash and pried open the housing, liberating a knot of cords. He pulled the cord again and the blinds smoothly rolled up the window, letting a flood of muddled gray light into the room.

He looked at her, not even trying to hide his triumph.

"Thank you," she said as her Blackberry hummed. She grabbed it and read quickly, her eyebrows lifting. "Sharon said the senator called again."

"Aren't you popular?" Arvo said, sitting in the side chair again.

She could see she would have to tell him something, and soon. She knew he wasn't leaving until he had his answer, and Abatha was due to arrive anytime. She sat at her desk and reorganized her notepad, pencils, and Blackberry. She wrote a few notes on the notepad, opened the manila case folder and rifled through some papers. She stood up and walked to the window to take in the view Arvo had made possible for her and learned why the blinds weren't open more often. The window view was filled with that awful apparatus of the gasoline refinery, clearly visible even through the dingy, unwashed glass. The refinery predated the school—how the school district could have thought this was a great place to build a schoolhouse was beyond her. Smoke poured from the towering smokestacks, accompanied by an occasional flame.

He decided to drop the bombshell on her. "Juney told me yesterday that there was another dead baby, years ago, found in almost the same place."

She didn't even flinch.

He got up and walked to her, close enough that he could speak in a low murmur. "They found both of them, right down from this window. The other case goes back twenty years. Never been solved. Juney says she has a crazy idea that the two cases are related."

Christine edged away from him until she found a comfortable distance. "Juney's got a reputation for her crazy hunches turning out not to be so crazy."

Arvo looked at Christine after she said this.

"Yes," she said, "The stories have made their way up six floors. You'd be surprised what we hear about you."

His eyes narrowed.

"Well, maybe not that surprised."

"Now, who's the one attempting humor?" he said.

"I wasn't joking," she shot back.

He wondered what she would look like smiling, an expression that wasn't likely to be seen on her face anytime soon. Christine Ivory had a concrete and sequential personality. He knew that in her line of work it was practically required in order to maintain sanity given the kind of patients she saw. Understanding this fact did not soften him towards her.

She turned and leaned on the window sill. "The girl may have nothing more for you than you already know."

"I won't know that for sure until I've had a chance to talk to her."

ARVO HEARD LIGHT FOOTSTEPS approaching the room. He turned and saw a fragile girl, who looked to be no more than eight or nine, judging by her size. One look at her face revealed the truth. The girl had the startled wild expression of a young bird of prey brought down by a poacher. She quickly composed her expression into a subdued look.

Seeing her was a shock Arvo hadn't anticipated. He felt Christine's eyes on him, taking the measure of exactly how this first interaction went. He knew she would judge now when she would give her approval for him to speak to her.

"Abatha, please come in," Christine said in an abrupt softening of her tone. One expected compassion from a healing professional. Arvo had heard it many times with the doctors and nurses he encountered throughout the criminal investigation process. Still, it surprised him, again, how caring Christine's voice sounded, as if she had some real human warmth. Here she'd turned it on with so little effort, as if it was her natural tone of voice. He often wondered why he never heard anything close to it when they spoke with each other. Except with her patients, Christine seemed to treat everyone, especially Arvo, like adversaries. Somehow she'd also made herself smaller, more approachable.

"This is Arvo Thorson, a detective with the county."

"Hello, Abatha," Thorson said quietly. He held out his hand to her, and to his surprise, she took it. He gave it the lightest of shakes and let go quickly, knowing he dared not take it any further. The girl seemed capable of flying off in a moment. Still, she managed to regard him calmly as if she were resting on his finger. Maybe that was the effect coming from Christine's warm, simple manner with her.

"Abatha, Mr. Thorson wants to talk to you about what happened when you found the baby. He is leaving now, but the two of us can talk about it today."

Abatha watched Christine speak and had no response.

"Detective, I'll call you later. Thank you for dropping by," she said, smiling lightly. He knew this came with the professional version of her and it meant nothing. Still, he'd seen it, it was a smile.

"I'll be expecting your call. Thank you for meeting with me today, Ms. Ivory." Christine closed the door on him without looking back.

Twenty minutes later, he arrived at his office not remembering any part of the drive that brought him there, whether he took the bridge under construction, or the detour. The whole way he was absorbed in wondering about that smile, where it could come from out of a woman who had never exhibited any feeling outside the confines of her therapy sessions.

Was it just her long training that taught her how to realistically appear to be capable of tender emotions—as a means to a successful patient outcome? Or was there something she recognized in her patients that called a different version out of her, even a memory of a more vulnerable version of herself? One that could almost be human. He shook the idea off. Criminals could fake it easily enough, gain some innocent victim's confidence and trust, and then take away everything. Christ, even Helen had proven herself more than capable in the art of emotional deception. Why wouldn't Christine be capable of the same?

He made his way down to his office, not even returning Juney's greeting as he bustled by. He reminded himself that Christine wasn't a criminal, and never would be. He wasn't remotely interested in getting anything personal from her. Thank God he only needed to see her occasionally when work demanded. So why was it so irritating to him that she smiled, so easily and beautifully, for someone she barely knew and then dismissed him coldly, as quickly as she could, whenever they were together? He shuddered, trying to get thoughts of the sweetly curving lips out of his mind. "Juney!" he summoned. "What's the status on that god damned coroner's report?" He pounded his fist on his desk, swearing again when thoughts of Christine's face floated back into his head.

8

"HOW ARE YOUR CLASSES GOING, Abatha?" Christine asked her young patient, whose clear, unemotional eyes focused somewhere outside the refinery-facing windows.

"Okay." Her eyes flickered momentarily on Christine's, and then looked around the little room, lighting on the empty credenza top.

Christine followed the girl's gaze as if it was a nearly invisible fishing line leading deep into a secluded, unexplored river slough. Something she threw out there would catch, she hoped. She wondered how long they'd both have to sit there, quietly waiting. Abatha was wearing her usual non-descript uniform of jeans and an oversized solid-color shirt. Her thin shank of hair was banded into a narrow single braid down her back, the only suggestion of a feminine person hiding inside her delicate frame.

"This place isn't much to look at, is it?" she offered. "I'm a neat freak, on the obsessive side. I brought my own cleaning supplies in since the school can't get to it."

The girl continued looking at the collection of dusty odds and ends. An overflowing garbage bag full of clothes lay in the corner of the room.

"To be honest, this room is going to be a challenge. I'm not sure I'm up to it." A vulnerability in the therapist sometimes helped patients to open up. "That bag of clothes, for instance. I'm just going to have to let that alone, I guess."

"Nobody wants any of those things," Abatha suddenly said.

"The clothes?" Christine felt the line tug. Careful now.

"They drop off used clothes here, but no one wants them."

"Oh," Christine said.

"Mr. Shenouda gets really annoyed about having to deal with the stuff that gets left here." She got up from her chair and walked over to the bag.

"Mr. Shenouda? Is he a teacher?"

"The janitor. He's complaining about the stuff all the time." She reached inside the bag and pulled out a piece of cloth. "See, it's dirty and torn. Why would anyone think someone would ever wear this again?"

"So, these are clothes people donate, or something?"

"I guess that's what they think. Mr. Shenouda calls them something else."

"Them? The people or the clothes?"

"Both sometimes." She gauged Christine's reaction to this remark before going on. Christine maintained a level of detached interest.

"I don't want him getting in trouble so I don't tell people exactly what Mr. Shenouda says to me."

Christine wondered more about what Abatha told Mr. Shenouda.

Christine joined Abatha next to the grubby bag. "May I," she asked, readying herself to plunge her hands into the bag. It was going to be hard without the rubber gloves.

"Go ahead."

Christine reached inside the bag, cautiously as if she might be bitten by whatever lay inside. She pulled out a pair of grimy, worn jeans, obviously unfit even for use as a rag. "I'm starting to agree with Mr. Shenouda's viewpoint."

"They tell him to leave the stuff here. Everything in this room is what they've told him to put in here."

"They?"

"The people, like the principal's secretary. She always says his name wrong when she tells him what to do with things like these clothes. She calls him Mr. ShenOWda, like as in 'ouch.' It's ShenOOda, just like in 'moon.' She never gets it right. She says, 'Mr. ShenOWda, put them with the rest of the things in the spare room.'"

Christine gingerly stuffed the jeans back into the bag.

"Mr. Shenouda calls it the 'throwaway' room. People think they've taken care of their business by putting things away out of sight."

So they had Christine meeting Abatha in a room of garbage everyone else was too busy to sort through. Leaving everything for someone else to work through later.

Meanwhile everyone just forgot and went on their business.

"So, these clothes will never get used by anyone, ever?"

"You see what they look like."

An idea came to Christine. "Can you help me with something? Maybe help Mr. Shenouda out a bit, too?"

"What?" The girl looked pleased, most likely by the thought of helping Mr. Shenouda out.

Christine stuffed the clothes deep into the bag, trying hard not to rip it. She knotted the plastic ends together and lifted it. It was going to be a struggle. Dirty, useless clothes were heavier than she thought. The citizens of Somerset Hills were filled with misplaced charity, obviously only lightening their consciences and occasionally their pocketbooks.

"How do we get to the dumpster?" She asked directly, the hint of conspiracy in her voice. She knew she couldn't overdo it. "Without being seen by anyone."

A girl whose best friend in the school was the janitor would know this, Christine was absolutely certain.

Christine thought she saw the tiniest glint creep into Abatha's eyes. Sunlight on a small cresting ripple. "Wait here," she said, opening the door and leaving silently.

Christine stood completely still, hoping no one would drop by to collect Abatha. She knew the appointment clock was ticking. She needed to have the girl in her 10:30 class and be driving back for another appointment soon. She knew she had plenty of time for both and did her best to quell her obsessing about schedules.

Abatha returned and led Christine down the hallway, away from the administrative offices. They took a shortcut through an empty early childhood education classroom. Christine was barely managing to hold the dead weight of the heavy plastic bag off the floor.

Abatha stopped as they came to another hallway, then they proceeded down, around a corner, and through an alcove that lead down some unused stairs. They came to a door marked "Emergency Exit Only."

"Won't an alarm go off?" she asked as Abatha pushed against the heavy door. It clicked open.

"It isn't working. Mr. Shenouda shut it off."

Christine dragged the heavy bag outside. Judging by the view of the refinery through the misshapen forest of stunted ironwood and chokecherry saplings, they were somewhere below Christine's temporary office. She followed Abatha along the edge of the building's foundation and around the corner, her heels catching in the soft ground. Close by, a couple of dumpsters sat near a loading dock. One had its lid open.

"Mr. Shenouda opened it for us," Abatha said.

Christine was learning not to be surprised about Mr. Shenouda's magical abilities with lost girls and dumpster lids.

Christine was panting and sweaty in her tailored jacket as she struggled to lift the heavy bag to the open edge. Abatha came to her side and maneuvered herself underneath, placing both hands over her head to push the bag up. It balanced on the edge of the dumpster's lip until Abatha gave one last jumping shove to send it over. It hit the bottom sending off a metallic thud.

Abatha noticed something near Christine's feet, and kneeled down.

"Here," she said, "this looks like yours."

A button had been ripped from Christine's suit by the garbage bag. She took it from Abatha and remembered that she had also heard a tear and felt it in the vicinity of her left arm hole. She took off her jacket to investigate. She could see daylight through the armpit.

"Kind of a mess," Abatha observed. "Maybe you should throw it in there, with the rest of the stuff."

"Oh, no," Christine said. "This I think can easily be repaired. I'll take care of it tonight."

They rested for a moment out of sight next to the building, but not out of sight of the sun, which warmed the foundation and lit the mousey gold strands in Abatha's hair. She didn't look too long at Abatha for fear of chasing her away, so instead sensed her standing close by. It seemed to Christine that Abatha had relaxed a part of herself, enough so that she took up more space than she had when she first arrived in the office.

"Mr. Shenouda will leave some cleaning things in the office, under the desk where no one will notice. He said that's as much as he can do without getting fired. He says he likes it when people clean up the goddamned mess." Abatha kicked a small stone underfoot. "He apologized to me for swearing. He always apologizes, even though I tell him I'm not bothered by it. Anyway, he said he's sorry the place is in such a mess. They don't let him clean it."

That was unexpected, Christine thought. She'd earned at least one ally today in Mr. Shenouda. She knew it was too soon to be certain of the depth of the alliance with Abatha.

They headed back to the door and Christine had a moment of concern. "Don't these things lock automatically from the outside?"

Abatha dug into her pocket and retrieved a key.

"Don't tell me. Mr. Shenouda?"

Abatha didn't identify her conspirator. When they arrived back at the office by a different, but still out of sight, equally circuitous route, there were only a few minutes remaining in their appointed time.

"That detective. What was his name?"

"Detective Thorson."

"When am I supposed to talk to him?"

"It's really up to you," Christine said.

"Who else will be there in the room when I talk to him?"

"Usually they don't want anyone else, if that's possible." There's no way to know how much even a trusted guardian can distract a child during an interview. Christine felt obliged to mention that the interview might be videotaped.

"Can I ask to have someone with me?"

Christine nodded.

"Would they let you be in the room?"

"Yes, I can be there if you request that I be there."

Perhaps she had won two allies in the small conflict she was waging, not the one she was fighting with Arvo Thorson, or the senator. The one she hoped would eventually conquer the secrets threatening to consume Abatha. She was certain there was more going on than the recent discovery's affect on her. Abatha's silenced, sturdy resolve told Christine that she'd surrendered her simple trust, long ago.

"Tell the detective that I want you in the room when he talks to me."

"I will tell him that."

An alarm buzzed on Christine's Blackberry, signaling the end of their appointment.

"Are you coming back tomorrow?" Abatha asked as she was leaving.

"Yes, I'll be here."

"Okay," Abatha said, sounding a little tired. She headed out but then stopped in the doorway and turned around to look at Christine again.

"Yes?" Christine asked.

"I'll let Mr. Shenouda know you'll be back."

"Thank you. I appreciate it," Christine said.

9

A FEW DAYS LATER, AND SOONER than she had ever thought would be possible, Christine was arriving at the county's crime witness interview room. The interview room wasn't at all like the ones seen in television crime dramas. Christine knew this from past experience accompanying young victims to their witness interviews. The TV rooms were dreary and harshly lit, with a nearly undisguised one-way mirror that no one could hide from, and apparently only accessible by a descent into some hellish, remote dungeon of an inner city police station. The Mendota County vulnerable witness interviewing area was in a spacious, airy wing of the courthouse. The room itself featured overstuffed side chairs, a small table, a few lamps lit with soft bulbs. The wallpapered walls were a soft, baby-blanket blue, with a border of friendly pastel-colored giraffes near the ceiling. A box of toys sat in one corner.

Christine knew that among the cuddly teddy bears were a few other toy-like dolls, probably in a cabinet. However instead of playing house with them, young victims of sexual abuse used the anatomically correct toys to reenact the bestial crimes committed against them. These were the types of interviews that left Christine shocked and drained for days after, and most clearly contrasted the pastel atmosphere of the room from the phony TV versions.

Abatha would not be using those toys today. She was here as a witness, not as the victim of abuse, though Christine still wondered if she had been victimized, at some point, in her short life. Christine and Abatha had met again the previous afternoon at Abatha's school. Together, they'd filled up a garbage bag of junk stuffed in the drawer of her desk and by the time it was full, Christine had snagged and ruined her hose after crawling behind a cabinet to retrieve some newspapers that had gotten jammed behind it.

Abatha showed her the way to an oversized garbage can, with less of the previous trip's subterfuge. On the way back, Abatha walked ahead of Christine, moving confidently and comfortably. Back in the office, she remained standing, articulating in an unreadable tone, "If you don't mind, I think I'll just go back to my class."

"It's okay if you want to stay, or go. Completely fine," Christine assured her.

"Don't take this the wrong way," Abatha began. "I really don't need you. I mean . . . I don't need this therapy stuff."

"Therapy stuff?"

Abatha smiled. "I'm sorry. I know you're trying to do a job. It's just that . . ."

Christine listened, hoping for the smallest advance. The narrowest window into the profound world where Abatha drifted, alone and in silence.

Abatha rocked in a light motion, rolling from her heels to the balls of her feet, then back, as if she were floating on an invisible boat. Her eyes lit on a corner of the ceiling. "I don't need to be here."

You mean you don't want to be here, Christine thought.

"You may feel like you don't need to be here," Christine said, thinking fast. "And that's really fine, but I have something to tell you, something we can keep just to you and me. A secret."

Abatha slowly stopped rocking and listened quietly.

"The time you spend here in this . . ." she smiled catching Abatha's eye ". . . pig sty . . . of an office isn't to help or serve me" Christine walked next to Abatha. "It isn't for the school, the teachers, and the principal." She knelt next to her, "or for your grandmother."

"It's just for you."

The girl focused on her face for once. Christine had received reports from Abatha's teacher that the girl was completing assignments well in class. She kept to herself, which was nothing new. So far the other kids weren't bothering her, considering all the publicity the crime had brought to the school. On the other hand, she'd observed no one approaching Abatha, to offer sympathy, or simply to be a friend to her. Still, Abatha didn't seem to be suffering from being a loner.

Signs, all good ones, but Christine knew they didn't provide the complete story of what might be going on in the girl's head.

"I want to talk to that detective. What was his name?"

"Arvo Thorson."

"Can I go and see him? I mean, tomorrow even?"

"Certainly. If you feel ready."

"Don't they need my . . . um . . . statement? Right away? I want to talk to the detective as soon as I can."

"I'll let the detective know."

"Okay."

"Can I ask you one more thing?"

The girl gazed at her, not exactly trusting, but at least accepting.

"Think about what I told you. This time that we meet together—it's just for you. What do you want, Abatha? What's been missing? Even if you don't know, I want to you to think about just you, and what you need. And not what you think anyone else needs from you. Okay?"

The girl considered what she said, but didn't answer. She turned to leave, but stopped, swiveling back around. "Will I see you tomorrow?"

"Yes. Of course."

"I'll tell Mr. Shenouda you need more paper towels."

Christine began to wonder whether she'd end up cleaning the entire school before she knew anything more about Abatha.

Aʀᴠᴏ ᴀʀʀɪᴠᴇᴅ ᴀᴛ ᴛʜᴇ ᴡɪᴛɴᴇss ʀᴏᴏᴍ half an hour after Christine did. She was early as usual, so he couldn't be blamed for the impatience she felt. It was still fifteen or twenty minutes before the scheduled interview start time.

"Is she here yet?" Christine asked Arvo.

"No." He sat down in the interviewer's chair. She sat off in a corner of the room. "They'll announce when she arrives, before bringing her in."

"I know how it works, Arvo. I don't need a lecture," she snapped, noticing again the ugly run down the hose on her right shin.

He looked ready to bite her head off for that comment. "Do you really have to start out this way? Again?"

"I apologize. That wasn't called for." She wondered if she should say more.

"That's a first. An apology from the high and mighty, perfectly dressed Ms. Ivory."

"I apologized, didn't I? I'm not sure why that deserves a sarcastic response from you." Christine didn't even attempt to hide her anger with a faked, relaxed pose. She sat with her arms folded across her chest, glaring openly at him.

"What's eating you, Christine? I'm tired of this attitude I always get from you. It never gets better. As unprofessional as I am, I know we still have a job to do here. Would you please get over whatever's making you such a bitch?" He held his arms out, completely overwhelmed by his lack of power over any of the women he interacted with in his life.

"Okay, I'll tell you. You know, you aren't the only one who keeps after me about this girl. I heard from the senator again. Her staff is preparing for an 'appearance' at Abatha's school. They want to drag her up onto the stage and make some kind of example out of her." She stood up and began stalking around the room. "It's all some stupid part of their family first agenda. It will do absolutely nothing for Abatha but harm her."

Christine rummaged through the drawers for a Kleenex. She knew her mascara had smudged when she accidentally rubbed an itchy eye. She felt the filth from the dirty office in every pore, and even when she took a shower after getting home from the daily sessions in that office, she never quite felt clean.

She found some tissues and jammed her finger in a drawer as she pulled a supply out. "Damn it!" She slunk back to her chair.

"I can't even stop them. The girl's crazy grandmother has given her blessing to the whole thing. It's set up for around six tonight. I wasn't exactly sure she was ready for this interview today, but I had to get her out of that insane environment they call a middle school over there."

Someone knocked on the door and announced Abatha had arrived.

"Get a grip on yourself," Arvo warned Christine. But his warning wasn't necessary, because the moment Abatha came into the room, Christine transformed herself. Once again, she was the soft welcoming healer. He couldn't believe it.

Arvo asked Abatha to sit down wherever she felt comfortable. Abatha scanned the room, having seen Christine immediately. She sat down in a chair directly opposite Arvo, her back to Christine. Christine knew it was because Abatha was here to give him whatever he wanted.

"ABATHA," ARVO BEGAN, "Thank you for coming in to talk to me."

Abatha said nothing, and only turned her watchful eyes to the camera she was exactly positioned in front of. Arvo saw the direction of her gaze.

"I believe Ms. Ivory told you that these sessions are recorded? You understand that?" Arvo didn't look at Christine, but knew she was watching him carefully.

Abatha answered clearly this time. "Yes."

"Let me explain the way the interview works first, and then we'll get started." Arvo suspected the girl was already clear on what was expected of her. Christine would have made sure of that, before giving her blessing. He also knew Christine would not have been in the room today without being directly requested. Christine went beyond merely following the rules. She often wrote them. He felt her across the room, still surprised how her demeanor changed. Did her patient have a stronger calming effect on her than she did on her patient?

"I'll ask you a lot of questions, beginning with some very basic ones, like who you are and how old you are. Then I'll ask you particular questions about what happened a week ago. Answer as best as you can about what you know and what you remember."

Abatha said, "I understand."

"Anytime you want, you can take a break. Just let me know. Ms. Ivory is here today for anything you need, too. She won't be asking any questions." He knew Christine would not interfere. Thankfully she was on professional autopilot now, and this type of interview did not require her particular skills.

The interview began. Arvo asked a series of simple questions, a laundry list of name, age, address questions that he already knew the answers to, but they established, for the purposes of the interview, that Abatha's identity was the same as the girl on a particular shore on a particular day.

They went slightly deeper. Arvo handled the shift to the more meticulous level of detail carefully. He knew that careful, gradual shading was required to move Abatha from the lighter to the darker aspects of her experience the day she discovered the baby.

He arrived at a crucial point in his questioning, after what seemed like an eternity to him, the pace telling him he was proceeding correctly. With caution. Given Abatha's age, any outcome was possible now. She might either freeze up, begin to lie, or go into hysterics. He knew Christine was monitoring every word he said now, how he sat in his chair, even the distance between each breath he took. Even though she was programmed not to interfere, he knew he couldn't count on that, not with Christine Ivory. He hoped that she would cooperate, that the room itself would cooperate, its quiet, camera eye casting a detached gaze on the proceedings.

"Abatha can you tell me what kind of day it was when you went outside on the 31st of August, if you remember?"

"Summery." She said simply, with no apparent change in her manner. "It was morning when I went out. I always go out in the morning, when it's cool. I like the feel of the dew on my feet." It was as if she was the one who led Arvo to this point in his questioning, calmly coaxing him along with a scattered trail of breadcrumbs. "I never wear shoes in summer."

This Arvo knew lined up with the crime scene notes and photographs. A set of girl-sized footprints, just the shallowest of depressions, leading up to the location where the baby lay in the water. Where the footprints turned away from the baby, the depressions from the toes were deeper, the heel prints hardly apparent. A few feet away, deeper rounded prints, perhaps from her knees collapsing into the position the girl was found in.

She began to tell him where she had walked that day, without requiring any further questioning from him. The dirt road she always walked, the one that went under a graffiti-filled railroad bridge as it descended to the river. The types of songbirds she saw along the way, and how the birds told her about the weather and time of year. The small animals she encountered each day, curious chipmunks, gray squirrels, rabbits, sometimes a fox, or rarer, a coyote slinking off.

"Close to the river, right where I come to River Road and have to decide which way to turn, I looked for the eagles. If they are sitting on the dead tree branches right on a small island, then I turn left. If they aren't there, I turn right."

"Which way did you turn that day?"

"I turned left."

That meant she headed upriver, where the main channel was narrow, with fast moving currents and quiet, cut off backwater channels that snaked across the flood plain.

"That part of the road goes right next to the river, and there aren't many houses, so it's easier for me to get down to the shore. I like both directions, so that's why I always let the eagles decide for me. When they're there, I like to visit."

Arvo walked along the road. Christine he knew wasn't far behind. They were following Abatha's memories of the day. It occurred to him that despite the fact that Abatha spent so much time alone, she wasn't lonely in the least. The companionship of the busy natural world seemed to be all the company she needed, or wanted. Fortunately for her, since she really had no other options, the natural world delivered everything she needed. Arvo wondered when and if she would ever get back there, now that a human drama and all of the consequences of resolving it had snagged her like a bird in a net.

"I could see the eagles perched on the treetops, and there is a place along the road where a narrow path takes you down to the river. There are a couple of big boulders there you can sit on, so I took that path when I came to it."

Arvo felt himself holding his breath. They were coming to another transition. He reminded himself to remain measured, because any sort of change inside the room might distract Abatha from this crucial part of recounting her story.

He wondered how much she remembered from the time after she arrived on the shore. "How long had you been out by then? Do you have any idea?"

"Um. I never wear a watch so I don't know. But usually, in summer, I go back home around lunchtime. Some days I even bring something to eat."

"Did you bring something with you that day?"

"No. I was supposed to go back and go school-shopping with Grandma."

"So it was still morning then?"

"Yes. The sun was in my eyes as I walked down the path to the river." Abatha stopped talking, and Arvo was sorry he'd interrupted her with his questions about what time it was when she arrived at the river. At this critical point in her narrative, Arvo needed every detail.

Throughout this whole telling of her story so far, Abatha's eyes had wandered around the room, just as they might during her daily walks wander through the brush, the fields, and the river bottom. She explored every detail, was alert to every sound, filled her lungs with the air that was sacred to her along the edge of the river and on the empty hilltops she roamed. Now, as her story took her, Arvo, and Christine to the edge of the water, she anchored her eyes on Arvo's face.

But he knew she wasn't seeing him.

"I got to the river and watched the eagles. One lifted off the tree, gathering huge gulps of air in its wings. First it went down river to the area where it widens, and I thought it might be headed down to Pine Bend, but then it turned and came back and close by it hovered overhead, it must have seen something in the water."

"I looked down too and followed its gaze down to the water. I didn't know what it might have been looking at and then I saw something in the corner of my eye, nearer to shore, close by. There's lots of interesting driftwood that gets trapped in certain parts of the river, especially after a flood. There were floods in June, and the water had come up to the edge of the road I walked on, but it was pretty much back to its usual level."

Her eyes were still fixed in the direction of Arvo's face, but she was staring at something beyond the room.

"I walked over to where I saw what looked like an odd piece of driftwood. At first I thought it was a stump ball, or some random piece of trash. It wasn't. I came as close as a few feet away from it, and I knew it wasn't anything I'd ever seen by the river."

Two tears formed, one in each corner of her eye. She continued.

"Sometimes I see dead animals wash up on shore. Especially in a year when there have been floods. I know that nature works in certain ways and it's unfortunate when animals die. It makes me sad. I leave everything I find just the way I find it, except for when I find a bird feather or a piece of egg shell. Those things I collect."

Two tears rolled down each cheek, opening a channel that had been blocked.

"When I come across road kill, I can't stand it. People are too careless speeding along and it makes me sick to see anything killed on the road. When I can, I'll haul whatever died on the road off to the side. I do that so that carrion-eating birds and animals don't get hurt doing what they need to do."

More tears slid down her face, slowly.

"Other times I find dogs running loose, too close to the road. I do what I can to chase them off, or if I can, I'll catch them and get them back to where they belong. I hate to see dogs getting run over."

She stopped again, only for a moment, and a long breath shuddered out of her. "I really can't remember what happened after I first saw the baby. I don't remember how long I was there until people came. But what bothers me the most, after everything, is that I didn't know what to do for it. So I didn't do anything."

Her eyes finally focused on Arvo, and remembering where she was, she looked down.

"Was I supposed to leave it there? Was I supposed to get it off to the side somewhere? Was I supposed to catch it and get it home where it would be safe? I didn't do anything, that's what really gives me nightmares."

She shook her head. "I didn't do anything," she said, her face reddening, a torrent of tears and cries finally escaping.

Arvo caught Christine's eyes to get her judgment on Abatha's ability to go on. He knew she could see his own wet eyes, but didn't care. He silently acknowledged Christine's relief at seeing the girl finally express some emotion. He knew he had her permission to continue.

Abatha's sobs quieted and she wiped her nose and eyes with the tissues Christine had quietly retrieved from a cabinet. "I wish there was more I could tell you, but that's all I remember."

"Do you mind if I ask just a few more questions?" Arvo asked gently.

Abatha nodded.

"Did you see anyone in the area?"

"No. I would have remembered that. I almost never see anyone the places I go. I prefer it that way."

"Did you hear anything that seemed unusual to you, anything at all?"

"Nothing. Generally if I hear people, or boats or cars, I go a different direction. I really like being alone and away from people."

"Do you remember seeing anything else in the area where you found the baby? Any objects, pieces of clothing, anything at all? Was there anything you saw on the baby—a blanket, anything else?"

Abatha thought for a while this time. She didn't have an instant answer.

"I remember something. Something flashed at me, right before I saw the baby. I think it actually might have been what I noticed first. I saw something shiny in the water."

She was thinking hard now. Arvo could see that her eyes were again focused elsewhere. He knew she would have to bring herself forward again to the same place that had caused her to breakdown.

"I walked in the direction of the shiny thing that looked stuck on a piece of odd shaped driftwood. Now I remember. That was what I saw first. Something that looked like a bracelet on a worn tree branch. When I got close I saw it was a narrow band of silver beads, doubled around the tree branch. It looked like there was a larger bead in the middle of it. That's when I realized what I was looking at. It was a bracelet, but not on a tree branch. I saw fingers, and then a small arm, and then I realized it was a baby. After that I don't remember."

Abatha stopped talking then. Her face was pale and deep gray circles hung under her eyes. Her head drooped in exhaustion. Christine rose from her chair and came to her side, dropping to her knees. Christine asked, in an open expression, if the interview could end, but Arvo needed no prompting from her.

"I think we can bring this to an end, now. Abatha you've been very helpful. I know this must have been very difficult for you."

Christine gently escorted the girl out of the room, leaving Arvo behind. Once the door had closed, he leaned forward, face in his hands, and sat there only for a moment, resting. He got up and shut off the tape, grabbed his jacket and headed back to his office. There was much to consider, and an event planned for Abatha at her school that evening. He was not sure how he, Christine, and most of all Abatha, were going to have the stomach for what lie ahead.

10

ARVO ARRIVED AT SOMERSET HILLS Middle School just after 6:00 p.m. The parking lot was jammed, as was a narrow side street leading to the lot, so he had to park at the bottom of the hill and across the county road, in the strip club parking lot. Chugging on foot back up the hill as fast as he could, he wondered again about the placement of a school so close to an adult entertainment complex. To say nothing of the effects of the nearby refinery and its accompanying stench.

Certain hot days, the combination of acrid refinery fumes and the more metaphorical stink of the King of Spades drifted up to the higher ground occupied by the innocents of Somerset Hills. The Somerset Hills citizenry had long since tuned out the blots on the landscape—those bothered by either the strip club or the refinery simply left town. The school busses were routed to enter the school grounds from the back side, away from the strip joint, and most of the school windows that faced the King of Spades had been painted over. This was the moral lesson the children learned from their school's placement in the landscape: turn your back on your problems, and you could gradually lull yourself into thinking they never existed. Problem solved.

The police were happy to ignore the debauched establishment by the river. As long as the bouncers managed the jealous boyfriends of the dancing girls and ejected the groping patrons not willing to pay for the goods, there was generally no need for a law enforcement presence. Vern Eide, the owner, was also astute enough to keep a few off-duty cops well paid to mind the premises and avoid unwanted attention from the rest of the department.

Despite his displeasure about the proximity of the club and the school, Arvo often found it his duty and pleasure to attend to detective business there. The place was a convenient location to meet informants and have dinner and drinks, complements of the house.

Arvo panted heavily as he made the last corner onto the school's front drive and squeezed through the crowd of vehicles. The uneven sidewalk was overflowing with satellite-dish covered vans emblazoned with network affiliate station logos. When Senator Jane Columbus-Powers spoke, she wanted everyone to listen, and her advance people made sure that everyone knew where and when she would be appearing. With the polls showing her reelection race closer than ever, dogged partly by questionable ethical issues that kept cropping up from her previous term, Columbus-Powers had to wring the votes out of every opportunity. Tonight, Arvo thought ruefully, she obviously had the audience she needed.

Arvo saw the entrance to the school gymnasium was packed. As he made his way to the double doors, he recognized a few heavy-set men he knew were bouncers from the King of Spades. He held out his hand to a giant of a man, but instead of a handshake, an arm immediately barred his way to the gymnasium.

"Invitation only," the gruff voice said.

"Oh, the public's not invited to this stunt?"

The bouncer frowned. "Sorry, Arvo, you need to show an invite."

"Here's my invitation," he answered, flipping open his wallet to flash his badge.

The bouncer spoke behind his hand to a shorter man who wore a wireless ear piece. The man with the blue tooth mumbled something into his phone. Then he nodded at the fat bouncer and the arm came down, admitting Arvo at last.

"Thanks, Jerry," Arvo said as he hurried through.

Inside the gymnasium, a small stage that usually featured children playacting fairytales in homemade costumes was covered with red, white and blue bunting and six enormous American flags. A simple and elegant podium, obviously not something from the ramshackle green room that housed the worn children's props, presided on the stage. Cables snaked across the floor and were held down with miles of duct tape. Arvo spied Abatha sitting center stage next to a wide-set older woman who looked robust but acted frail. Margaret Cox had made herself up for the occasion, her rouged cheeks, sharply penciled brows, and glossy lipstick were camera-ready, and she smiled in anticipation of her moment of fame. Abatha stared at someone at the side of the audience. Arvo followed the target of her eyes confident he knew exactly who she was homing in on. It was Christine, standing off to the side of the main audience, next to the school kitchen, which had temporarily been converted into Jane Columbus-Power's dressing room.

Christine briefly averted her eyes from Abatha's to acknowledge Arvo's presence, then went back to anchoring Abatha. Arvo had to admit he was glad she'd gotten to the school in time. He saw her simple elegant dress wasn't exactly tight, but somehow hugged her curves in a tasteful way that allowed him to acknowledge that she had a certain beauty, though she wasn't at all his type. He walked to her side.

A woman in a plain gray suit came up and spoke briefly to Christine. She turned to Arvo and said, "An appearance has been requested."

"With who?"

"The senator wants to talk with both of us."

"Can we send our regrets?"

"We could, but then they'll come for us anyway."

As they squeezed their way through the packed room following the suited woman, Arvo realized that with the exception of Christine, Abatha, and the fat bouncer from the strip club, he hadn't recognized anyone in the crowd.

He spoke into Christine's ear. "Have you seen anyone you know here? Aside from Abatha?"

She shook her head. "I noticed that right away."

"They must have bussed people in. If she's that unpopular, I wonder why she's even in a tie at this point."

They were led through the small, cramped middle school kitchen until they reached an area by a couple of huge freezers. There stood the senator circled by a half dozen advisors, many with phones plastered to their ears and flashing Blackberries on their hips.

The senator was smaller than Arvo thought she'd be, given her powerful stature on the national scene. Attired in a beautifully tailored, expensive-looking scarlet suit (Christine told him later it was a Valentino suit costing thousands of dollars), she had the delicate complexion of a bone white dagger handle. "I'm delighted to meet you at last," she said, her arm cutting in front of Arvo to grasp Christine's hand.

"This is Detective Thorson," Christine said, gesturing towards Arvo.

"Detective," she said, accenting the last syllable upward sharply. "I am glad to see the both of you here on this occasion."

Arvo could clearly see this was not the case. There would be much required of anyone to gain Senator Columbus-Power's true appreciation.

"I don't approve of your involving Abatha in this public relations scheme." Christine said.

"I'm certain you don't, Ms. Ivory. But soon you'll see the benefit of tonight's presentation. That is a charming dress you're wearing, by the way. I haven't seen anything like it this year."

"Stop with the bullshit, Senator." Arvo butted in.

"Are you saying you don't approve of Ms. Ivory's taste? It's uncanny how she's coordinated everything so well."

"I'm not talking about Christine. Who are all these fake constituents you've got out there waiting to cheer you. Where'd you bus them in from this time? The next state? Or maybe they travel around with you on your private jet."

"Now, Detective, there's no reason to insult me, my staff, or the fine people attending this event."

"I'm not insulting Ms. Ivory."

"Detective," Senator Columbus-Powers said with a blade-sharp voice, "your estimation of the electorate's intelligence is shameful. To suggest that the people out there are not my supporters is absurd."

"I'm not *suggesting* anything." Arvo felt ready to throttle the woman.

Christine inserted herself. "Senator, I don't know what you plan to say out there. But if I see that girl becoming harmed in any way that compromises her healing, believe me I'll find a way to make you take responsibility."

"Christine. Please understand that what we are here to do tonight is only intended to help the situation for her and others like her." She went on in a more insinuating tone. "The sheriff told me how passionate you are," she said. "That you would go and in fact have gone to great length for your patients' welfare."

Christine's eyes widened. What could the senator have possibly heard about her?

"Yes. It's commendable to see a strong, capable, and beautiful woman like you doing what's necessary to achieve results, especially when what's required sometimes may put you at professional risk." Senator Columbus-Powers stroked the bottom of her lip as she said this.

Christine knew that her own record was spotless, but began to wonder what a powerful woman like the senator could do to her. If she wanted to.

"I think we understand each other, don't we? We're two of a kind."

Christine felt Arvo's hand on her shoulder. He knew she was about to take her first professional risk, and not the kind the senator was insinuating with her carefully positioned remarks.

One of the senator's assistants tapped her shoulder. "They're ready."

"Again," the senator said taking her leave, "I appreciate that you are a part of the audience tonight. We've some interesting news to share that affects the two of you and that poor young girl out there." She walked out with her entourage.

As Christine and Arvo attempted to follow her, they were blocked by several of her staff and the crowd, which had gotten larger during the time they were in the kitchen. Arvo elbowed a path through for himself and Christine, and they found a place by the wall where Abatha was again able to seek out Christine's watchful eyes.

"I wish I had a drink," Arvo muttered in Christine's ear. "It might keep me from trying to kill that woman."

"I probably need one, too. But I'm pretty sure it wouldn't help keep me from wanting to take my first professional risk."

"What the hell was that about anyway?"

"Obviously her making it known she can do anything she wants—at any time and to anyone." Christine shuddered.

The senator made her way to the stage amid the loud cheers of the audience, none of whom anyone in town would have recognized, with the exception of some school officials and Abatha and her grandmother, and even then they were only recognized because their faces had been plastered all over the news.

The senator thanked and quieted the audience, and went on to thank the school principal and the members of the school board for allowing her to come speak at the school that evening.

"I'm here tonight to talk to everyone about the importance of the values of fine, hardworking people like those of you gathered here tonight. And what happens when we let bad moral choices get in the way of what's right. I'm talking about a terrible crime that was discovered just a week ago, and by one of our own from Somerset Hills."

She gestured to Abatha.

"Because of someone's terrible choices, this innocent child was made to see things that no one should ever see, especially not a young person like her, nor anyone else."

Abatha kept her eyes on Christine's. Christine wondered what might be going through her head.

"What can we learn from such a terrible crime as the murder of an innocent baby? I'm here to tell you tonight that I will not rest until we change the conditions that could have resulted in such a tragedy. And tonight we can begin to look at those conditions and plan the road ahead."

Christine braced herself. She wondered how long Arvo could keep his anger in check.

"We just learned, this very evening, that there has been an arrest in the case."

Christine turned to Arvo. "What?"

"News to me."

"This will come as a shock to all of the good, hard-working people of Somerset Hills. Unnamed sources have told our local media that a nineteen-year-old, unwed, illegal immigrant has confessed to having a baby in the past week and that baby can't be found anywhere. The young woman has been taken into custody."

Sounds of alarm and disgust came from the audience.

"Now while we are not here to render the verdict on the young woman, our office is not shocked by the allegations. It is, instead, a reminder that our journey during this campaign season, and indeed over the past six years, is just and honorable. We have consistently defended working Americans with humble family values."

Applause and cheers broke out, which the senator acknowledged with a slight bow of her head, and a smile.

"Our office has consistently led the way to keep the culture and tradition of towns like Somerset Hills as they are, and keep the jobs, like those at the refinery and the stockyards and the packing houses, in the hands of American citizens, and not illegal aliens who have no right to be here."

Abatha's face was growing pale, and it was clear that even her grandmother was dismayed by what she'd gotten both of them into. Christine was praying that the speech would be over soon.

"In closing, we are here tonight to thank all of you who have supported our vision and understand that while the road is long, our cause is just, and our vision of the future of Somerset Hills will come to pass. Thank you for attending."

The senator waved to the cheering audience and flashing cameras. Arvo turned to Christine and both began pressing forward to the side of the stage where Abatha sat pinned like a rare animal on display. They got to her side just as the senator took Abatha's hand, cameras flashing and clicking to capture the moment. Abatha drew her hand away as quickly as she was able, staring at it as if it were burned. Christine could see the child was trembling.

Christine grabbed Abatha and pulled her away. "The child has had enough for one night."

"As you wish, my dear," the senator said. "Thank you, all of you, for attending."

This time, Christine led everyone down the back hallway that Abatha had shown her over the past week. Mr. Shenouda was waiting for them by the emergency exit. He held the door open and let them out quickly, closing the door and locking it when they had gotten through.

He guarded the door, and even though he was barely five feet tall, he was ready, willing and able to take on all anyone that came looking for Abatha.

"Where's your car?" Arvo asked Margaret. She pointed out an ancient Plymouth station wagon. People were heading to their cars, and Arvo urged the group next to him to stay hidden behind the school.

"Where are your keys?" Arvo asked next.

Margaret dug through her vast, stuffed purse and extracted an enormous bundle of keys on a macramé key chain. She placed them in Arvo's outstretched hand, pointing out the one for her car.

Mr. Shenouda appeared at Abatha's side.

"Can you get everyone down the hill, taking some route that'll keep them out of sight of the crowd?" he asked Mr. Shenouda.

"There's an old set of stairs that goes through the woods here," he said, gesturing behind everyone.

"Good. Wait behind King of Spades."

Mr. Shenouda nodded and took Margaret's arm. Abatha held her grandmother's hand and they quickly made their way into the darkness.

"I'll be right behind you," he said as loud as he dared. "Christine, go get that station wagon and make your way, quietly, to the Club. Take the River Road and stay out of sight."

He handed the jangling keys to her and hustled after Mr. Shenouda.

Christine's heart pounded. She hurried to the car, looking around her to see if anyone noticed her. Fortunately a group of reporters was crowding around the senator and her entourage, just emerging from the school. Christine struggled with the keys trying to get the right one into position, and as she juggled huge mass, the unwieldy pile finally fell out of her hands.

"Shit."

She broke a nail retrieving the key ring and fumbled again trying to find the right one that would open and start the car. Finally she located it and she was inside, cranking the ignition, and grateful to hear it starting up. She made her way out of the parking lot, winding around the back to avoid being seen. Once she was out, she drove in the opposite direction from the club, zigzagging through a small neighborhood near the school and finally making it to River Road. She drove a mile and finally reached the club, driving around the back where everyone was waiting.

She got out and left the engine running.

"What took you so long?" Arvo muttered.

"I took the route you told me," she said, her nerves shot.

"That's right," Arvo said. "Sorry."

Arvo helped Abatha and her grandmother into the car. They drove off into the darkness of River Road without saying another word, and Mr. Shenouda was gone an instant later, making his way back up the hill to the school.

Arvo and Christine stood together watching the taillights of the Plymouth bobbing in and out on the curving road that headed to the trailer court where they lived. Even after the lights could no longer be seen, they stood in awkward silence. Arvo felt for his cigarettes, and remembering he no longer carried any, dropped his hands to his sides.

"Well . . ." Christine started to say, then didn't.

"That was even worse than I thought it'd be," Arvo said.

Christine began to feel her heart quieting down. "You really didn't know anything about that girl? The one they arrested?"

"I don't even know . . . where to begin on that question. I'm in complete shock, and at the moment I don't believe it."

"The sheriff said nothing to you?"

"Nothing. I tried to call him half a dozen times already, while we were waiting here. Tried Juney too, but she generally doesn't answer her phone at night."

An intoxicated couple stumbled around the corner to where Arvo and Christine were standing, the man's hand stroking the woman's buttocks, his lips on her neck. The man wore a silky shirt that had already become completely untucked and the women's skirt was already hiked halfway up her hips, encouraged by the groping hand of her escort.

"Excuse us," Christine stammered.

"Oh. Sorry. Didn't know shomeone was here already." The man barely stopped sucking on the woman's neck to notice them.

They staggered off in the direction of a dark clump of shrubs, shoving their way through the undergrowth and disappearing. Christine thought he heard the woman giggle in a nervous, apologetic way.

"I'm praying that Abatha is going to come out of this escapade unscathed," Christine said in an embarrassed tone.

"I think she'll be fine . . . especially since supposedly we now have the murderer in custody." Arvo looked in the direction of the shrubs, then turned awkwardly back to Christine, clearing his throat.

"Well. I hope so. That had to be traumatic. And it's obvious her grandmother is completely useless."

They could hear, clearly, the soft murmuring of the couple, the sounds of clothing being removed, and the hush of the night air.

"Well I suppose . . . Say—" he started, "—do you want to stop and . . . well not here, but somewhere else . . . have a little drink? Decompress?"

"Um. No." Christine heard the woman gasp sharply. "I meant not tonight," she said, louder than she needed to. "No, I meant . . . oh, damn, I don't care what I meant. I need to get out of here." She started off, then stopped abruptly, not more than ten steps away, her back to Arvo.

"Can I give you a lift back to your car?" he offered, trying not to sound like he might be gloating, even slightly, because she had to take him up on his offer. Especially in those heels she was wearing.

She swiveled around, and looked at him with irritated resignation.

"Yes. Thank you," she said politely, though it was clear she hated that she needed him.

He escorted her to his car, tipping his hand at bouncers on the way by the club's entrance.

When they were approaching his car a few moments later, she thought she heard a slow, soft wolf-whistle. She never remembered feeling as defeated by the sound of a man's appreciation, as she did that moment. She couldn't wait to get home, out of her filthy clothes, and into something, anything else, as long it was clean and untouched by the filth she felt clinging to her. She wasn't sure she could ever wear the outfit the despicable Senator Columbus-Powers found so charming, ever again.

Arvo dropped Christine off in the school parking lot, watching her until she had driven away. Thankfully the senator, her entourage, and all of the television crews had finally left. Only a few cars were left in the parking lot. Arvo sat in his dark car, the engine running. He ran his hands over his face.

He knew he and the sheriff had a reckoning coming the next day. Something just wasn't right about this girl being arrested, and him knowing nothing about it. What had he missed? He'd never had a case go the way this one had—the late interview of the witness, the lab tests taking forever, a U.S. senator mucking up everything. In his almost twenty years, he had never seen so many aspects of a case entirely so out of control.

He relaxed his grip on the steering wheel, his hands aching from the constant level of tension. His jaw hurt from constant clenching and he suspected he was grinding his teeth in his sleep, and pretty sure he'd chipped a crown. He loosened his tie and leaned back, licking his lips, suddenly feeling incredibly thirsty. He could taste the whisky he knew he'd be drinking as soon as he arrived home. He threw the car in drive, already planning the series of drinks he figured he'd earned from the day. The list was not too different from any other day, he would have realized, had he forced himself to think about it. Maybe . . . the drinking? His drinking? Did it have something to do with how poorly this case was going? He should think about that, he really should. Definitely tomorrow he would think about that. Tonight, he just needed a drink. Or two.

PART 2
MISSISSIPPIBOI

11

THE NEWS ABOUT THE BREAK in the case traveled lightening fast through Somerset Hills and like everything else around Arvo lately, he could not keep up, no matter how fast he sped on his way to the office the next day. He was furious that he'd been the last to know, and he was ready to face down the sheriff, the one man who had obviously been keeping important details about the case from him.

Unfortunately, he would have to endure a hastily called press conference first. A press conference he had not been invited to. The microphones were lined up outside the county offices, and Arvo saw the same reporters and camera operators he'd seen at the middle school the night before.

The sheriff, Bill Ruud, a long-time fixture in Mendota County, won election after election, often running unopposed. He was in his late fifties now, his face as wrinkled as the uniform he'd worn for most of his two decades in office. He was just finishing a brief statement when Arvo arrived.

"When was the arrest made?" a reporter shouted.

"The suspect was brought in late yesterday afternoon."

"Is she going to be released soon?"

"She isn't going to be released. She's being held without bail, due to existing immigration issues."

"What can you tell us about the information that led to her arrest?"

"I can only tell you that some significant information came to our attention only yesterday morning, which led us to bring in the person of interest."

"We've heard she's a nineteen-year-old illegal named Maria Vasquez. Can you confirm that for us?"

"Yes, I can confirm that."

Arvo wondered how all of this substantial information was getting out, and without him, the lead investigator, knowing anything about it.

"We have several sources telling us that Miss Vasquez was recently a patient in Riverridge Hospital, admitted after she was weakened from hemorrhaging, like the kind that might follow a birth. Do you have any information that would corroborate this story?"

Sheriff Ruud held up his hands. "As the investigation is ongoing, I can't comment on that."

"What do you know about Miss Vasquez's boyfriend? It's been reported that he has fled the area, and possibly the country."

"We're actively working to bring Mr. Fernando Rios in for questioning. We've issued a warrant for his arrest."

"What sort of condition is Miss Vasquez in?"

"Miss Vasquez's doctors say that she's weak, but recovering." With that Sheriff Ruud stated that the press conference had come to an end. The reporters attempted to ask a few more questions, but Bill headed inside, ignoring them, spotting Arvo opened the door to county building.

"Arvo, just the man I need to see. Come, we'll go to my office." The sheriff held the door open for him, and Arvo entered suspiciously even after the sheriff gestured him inside.

As they walked in and through the courthouse atrium, their footsteps echoed on the polished tile floor. The place was deserted except for a few clerks and secretaries putting in early hours before the crowds arrived to renew their licenses or make their court dates.

"Bill, I need an explanation!" Arvo shouted when they got to the elevator. "What in the hell is going on? With *my* case!"

"Arvo," the sheriff said in a low voice, punching the up button and waiting for the echoes from Arvo's voice to quiet. "We'll talk about this when we get to my office."

They got into the elevator and Arvo felt himself steadily reddening.

This morning he wished Christine had taken him up on his offer to have a nightcap. It might have prevented the headache he had from the booze he went home and drank himself. Maybe the hangover was the only thing keeping him standing in place now.

They arrived at the sheriff's fifth-floor suite. As they walked by his secretary, she gave Arvo the same lovestruck look she always did and that he never followed up on.

"Dawn, hold my calls," the sheriff said, politely holding the door open once again for Arvo.

Once inside, he gestured to a chair and shut the door behind them. Arvo thought he heard the sheriff lock it, but he knew it was only hangover paranoia.

The sheriff came and sat down ceremoniously at his desk, clasped his hands together, and looked Arvo in the eye.

"What the hell is wrong with you?" he said.

"What the hell is wrong with me?" Arvo said. "What's going on with this case? *My* case."

"That's exactly what I'd like to know," the sheriff responded. "For fuck's sake, Arvo. Every time I see you lately, you're either drunk or hung over, sometimes both. A major break in *your* case that you don't know anything about. What you do get done, is done late. And you never file paperwork."

Arvo felt like he'd been struck.

"What is this about, Bill?" Arvo would have shot out of his chair with rage except that he was really more bothered by being scolded by the man who he'd respected as a father and loved like a brother. The words hurt more than he wanted to let on. "And since when are you so by the book?"

"Arvo, we both go back a long way. And I know you've seen me through some pretty rough times."

Arvo remembered driving Bill home the many nights he was too drunk to drive during those few months that his wife lay dying in a hospice.

"Everything else I can set aside and pretty much turn a blind eye to. But when you lose control of a case so much that the break comes in and you don't even know about it? And then, I get some toady from the senator's office calling me threatening to press assault charges against my best detective."

"Assault charges! What?"

"Yes. I received a call this morning about your conduct at the school last night."

"I did nothing."

"There were witnesses."

"They're lying! You know those kind of people as well as I do. Everything they say is marketing bullshit for their campaign. They're the ones who should be charged with endangering that kid. What the hell was that stunt about last night?"

Arvo finally leapt up and paced to the window, raking his hands through his hair and pulling out a few strands in the process.

"Arvo. For your own good, I want you to come and sit down and I want you to calm yourself down, man, before you give both of us coronaries."

Arvo sat down, still furious, but trying to do as he was told.

The sheriff leaned back in his chair, observing Arvo patiently for a few moments.

"I think you should take some time off."

Arvo shot a look at him.

"Look, I know you don't want to hear this but you'll hear it from me. Arvo, you have a problem. Now maybe it's temporary and when more time has passed after the divorce—"

"—this has nothing to do with the divorce. Can we stick to what's happening to my case?"

"—but that's just it. Everything related to your professional work, if that's what we stick to, as you suggest, has gone to hell. You know it, Arvo."

"No. I don't know it. I just interviewed Abatha yesterday. I mean, for chrissakes, Bill, the coroner's report isn't even in yet, unless someone hasn't informed me about that and you'd be damn sure Juney wouldn't keep that from me."

"No. The coroner's report hasn't come in."

"So we've got a dead baby, dead we don't know how long. Exactly what killed it we don't know. We've got one witness, a kid. And all of a sudden we've got some Mexican girl who turned up in a hospital showing signs of a recent birth and two of those three are now connected and the case is closed? Is that it?"

"No one's saying it's as simple as that. Jesus H. Christ, Arvo. Let's look at the facts as I see them. And please, take an honest look at yourself and draw your own conclusions." He took a breath and Arvo sat back.

"I've got my top detective looking everyday like he's being dragged through shit, smelling of booze, barely able to get himself into the office."

Arvo shook his head. "Yes, I know I'm in horseshit shape. But we both know that I'm not messing up on this case. Something else is going on here, I'm sure of it. Like who for instance got the tip on that girl? Who else is involved here?"

"I was told the tip came in with some info from an investigation being done on the federal level. We're following up on it. That girl definitely had a baby, and the baby's missing." The sheriff's patience was wearing thin, even with his old friend.

Arvo couldn't believe what he was hearing. The investigation was taking the flimsiest evidence, and hanging the whole case on it, involving not just one innocent person in Abatha, but now some poor girl who probably barely spoke a word of English and had been hauled in for no particular reason but just the fact of an unsubstantiated connection to a personal circumstance.

"Well, for chrissake, Bill. Why don't we just haul in every woman in the county who just had a baby and line 'em up. Why this girl?" Arvo was growing hoarse from the combination of poor sleep and shouting.

"Arvo you're forcing me to tell you what I wish I didn't have to tell you," the sheriff said. "You're off the case. You're on leave."

"No! You can't do that! Bill, I'm telling you you've got it all wrong." Arvo's voice finally cracked and he couldn't go on.

"I'm sorry, but you're going to have to leave this office now, Arvo. I know it sounds like a cliché, but I really do mean it. Take a break and get your act back together." The sheriff walked to the chair Arvo sat in, his fingers gripping the upholstery so hard his nails were starting to tear into it.

"Come on, Arvo. It's time for you to go home for a while."

Arvo left the office and stood in shock next to the secretary's desk.

"Can I do something for you?" she asked, though it was obvious Arvo wasn't listening.

"The sheriff had them put some paperwork together for you."

He looked at her mutely as she spoke to him.

"Look, I'll walk with you, we can stop by HR and get the papers. If you want, I can explain what you need to do."

In the haze of spent rage, it dawned on him she might be trying to hit on him. She wasn't bad looking, for a homely secretary. And he knew he was nursing a grudge against her boss.

"Sure. What the hell. Show me to HR. I've got nothing else to do. As long as you're free. We'll get an early lunch, too, while we're at it."

She grabbed her purse and called to the sheriff to let him know she was going to lunch and not sure when she'd be back. Later, she had enough sense to drive Arvo, once again besotted, home.

Though she had hoped for much more from their first date, she learned quickly how little there was of him to give. So she left him half dressed, passed out in his own bed, alone.

12

IT WAS GETTING CLOSE TO NOON on a Friday, and Christine hadn't even mustered the courage to look in her closet. Her schedule had suddenly opened up in the days after the announcement that a suspect had been arrested in the death of the baby. Her appointments with Abatha continued for the time being, and they attended to little else than going through the junk in the temporary office at the school.

Then Abatha's grandmother called Thursday to say the girl wouldn't be coming to school Friday, something vague about an infection, and the rest of her Friday calendar opened up due to other unexpected cancellations. Christine called in and took the day off, catching Sharon off guard with a half-baked, mumbled excuse.

She shuffled through her spacious, tastefully color-coordinated condominium to her designer bathroom and looked at herself in the ornate, oval mirror. For the first time in a long time, she had no idea what to do with her hair either.

She dragged herself back to her kitchen, poured herself the last of the coffee, and slipped through a sliding glass door to her deck. For a mid-September day, it was still surprisingly warm. Hints of fall colors were starting to show in the river hills. A lone eagle flew high above the river. Christine's view was one of the best in town, well downriver from the refinery and around from Great Cloud Island, so from her deck, she looked across a wide expanse of water, seeing all the way to the undeveloped bluffs on the west side of the river, and far beyond. A dozen empty barges were anchored on the other side of the river and a tug was pushing four loaded barges upstream to the capital.

Her stomach growled. She'd had little to eat for breakfast and knew there was even less she was interested in having for lunch. There was nothing to do but pull on something, somehow, and head out to a restaurant, and one where she could be sure of not being recognized. She didn't want to be seen in the uncoordinated, slopped together ensemble she was sure she'd be wearing.

She pulled on a pair of plain Levi's, a gray, silk t-shirt, and a knit cap over her unwashed hair. She rummaged through a drawer for an oversized pair of sunglasses. She didn't bother to drag lipstick across her mouth. She was about ready to head out when she made one concession to hygiene. She brushed her teeth.

The phone rang as she was leaving and she scanned the caller ID. Her mother. She knew she owed her mother a visit this weekend, and she was dreading it as usual. Despite her typical pattern of not leaving things undone (the reason she and her secretary, Sharon, got along so well), she ignored the phone and left.

She drove north along a curving road that passed by the expensive houses on the southern edge of the town. As she went farther north, the surroundings got steadily older and poorer: an uneven arrangement of aging houses, shabby apartment buildings, decrepit gas stations, and abandoned storefronts were scattered along the way. Finally she passed the refinery and approached Abatha's school. She sank down into her seat, hoping no one at the school happened to be out. She passed the lumber yard and crossed over to the next town. She drove another couple of miles and saw a small café with a bold sign advertising simply, "GOOD FOOD." She parked and went inside.

A small, out of the way, corner booth was open, and she took it quickly, grateful for the darkness of the place. She hadn't been seen yet by anyone she knew, and she wanted to keep it that way. She ordered the "breakfast special, with everything," not even blinking at the amount of cholesterol she might be ingesting.

Someone had left a recent *People* magazine behind, and she opened it starved for news about other people's problems. Problems she didn't have to solve. She didn't even have to care if *People* decided to pin the blame on other *People* and not take any responsibility.

The breakfast special arrived just as she was reading about the latest detox/boyfriend/plastic surgery/arrest. She looked up to thank the waitress and she saw him, out of the corner of her eye, at a table on the other side of the restaurant. It was Arvo Thorson slouching over a newspaper, a bowl of half eaten cornflakes, and a sloppy coffee cup. His waitress arrived with a fresh pot of coffee suddenly blocking her view of him. She grabbed her sunglasses and jammed them on her nose, scraping the bridge hard. Obviously he had been there awhile. Maybe he hadn't seen, or recognized her.

When the waitress stepped out of the way she casually looked over to see if he had noticed her. He was stirring some fake creamer into his coffee by swirling his cup. He went back to his paper, seemingly unaware that a woman was watching him from across the room. She wondered whether he was faking his lack of awareness. She knew him enough to know that Arvo was more alert, even when hung over, than most people were completely sober.

She decided not to care whether he knew she was there or not. She turned to the next story in the *People* magazine and absorbed herself in a Princess Diana conspiracy theory.

"Slumming?" he said, managing to cause her to knock over her coffee cup. Arvo slid in across from her, smiling and holding his cup up to signal the waitress.

"Thanks, Betty," he said, tipping his head towards Christine. The waitress quickly wiped up the puddle of coffee threatening to run down onto Christine's Levis and refilled her cup too.

"You probably thought I didn't recognize you at first. What, by the way, is that you're wearing? Although I have to say that ensemble suits you better than what you usually wear. I like it, Christine. It makes you look almost approachable."

She frowned at him. "I'm not surprised you hang out in this place."

"There's nothing wrong with it. It's a great place. Good food, just like the sign promises. They know me and expect nothing from me but that I pay my check and leave a reasonable tip."

"I haven't seen you lately. Not that I want to see more of you. You're looking as terrible as usual."

He smiled. "There's a reason. That you haven't seen me, I mean."

"The baby case is all wrapped up, you mean?"

"Some would think that. Not me," Arvo answered, taking a gulp of his coffee. He paused longer than necessary, wondering if it was worth the bother to tell her. Would a small omission do anything for his pride, not that there was much of that left these days.

"I've been ordered to take a personal leave. And I'm off the investigation."

"You're not serious. Really?" Christine sounded obviously shocked. Even concerned. She was wearing a different attitude, not just a change of clothes. Unless she had Arvo fooled.

"Both are true. The sheriff said he was fed up with my generally inept handling of my life, the investigation, pretty much everything." He set his cup down and stared out the window. "For once, he and my ex-wife are in complete agreement about everything."

He felt Christine's eyes examining him. He wondered if she was diagnosing his problem. Nothing she could come up with would shock him. The short list might have been something along the lines of over-blown ego, alcoholism, depression, and bad husband. Also a terrible dresser.

"Has he said when you can return to work?"

"Um, nope. It's completely open-ended. I'm told I need to see a shrink, get some counseling, and then get a medical release before I can return. You don't happen to have a prescription pad handy in your pocket do you?"

She ignored the question. "Are you seeing a therapist? Not that I'm prying or anything."

"Why, do you have someone you'd recommend?" He said, taunting her.

"Absolutely not me," she said without much energy in her voice. "Not that I mean anything by that."

"Because we know you can't stand me. Not that I care," he qualified.

"Even if I did treat adults, which I avoid, I know too much about you and we have a history—"

"—of treating each other like shit."

"—of a general lack of respect for each other. Right?" she said, not sounding very sure of her logic.

He locked his eyes on her. "Right."

Betty came by with a broom, which gave them both an excuse to not say anything for several minutes. The place had cleared of the lunch crowd, stockyard kill floor managers in stained coats, cattlemen on their way back out of town with empty cattle trucks, a traveling salesman or two between appointments. They were all gone, leaving Betty to clean up before her 2:00 p.m. closing.

After she finished with her broom, she returned with two plates and half an apple pie. "On the house," she said. She left and returned with a dish holding a few scoops of homemade ice cream.

"Have you tried Betty's pie?" Arvo asked Christine.

"No thanks," she said.

"Come on," he said, dishing her up despite her objections. "You won't find better anywhere, and it'd be an insult to Betty to turn your nose up at it. And the ice cream," he said, dumping a huge melting blob of it on top of her pie slice, "is the best on the planet. Trust me."

Christine took at taste and she immediately spoke. "Well, for the first time ever, I can say I completely agree with you. It's delicious."

"Well, that is indeed a first."

Not another word was spoken until both dessert plates had been emptied and Betty effusively praised.

Christine fell back against the booth, smiling. Arvo saw a questioning, evaluating look in her eye.

"Spit it out. Be honest with me, Christine. This is the closest I'll come to therapy." He threw his arms forward in a mocking gesture of pleading. "Diagnose me, Ms. Ivory, healer of children."

"Are you sure?"

"Why the hell not? Nothing can hurt you after you've had Betty's pie."

"Well, for starters, you don't listen."

"Kid stuff. Try harder."

"You have a problem with authority."

"Boring."

"Borderline alcoholic."

"Come on. Borderline? I guess I'm not trying hard enough."

"Borderline. Underlying depression."

"Oh, come on, I'm practically falling asleep. Next you'll tell me I had an authoritative, emotionally unavailable father."

"You obviously aren't really interested in what I think," she said, pushing away from the table. "If you've got it all figured out, why are you asking me?"

"Come on, Christine. What, you're already quitting? I'm hardly even trying to fight you. You've seen worse from me."

She appraised his remarks.

"I'll shut up. Really. Go ahead."

Christine considered his remarks and watched the oily bubbles float around in her coffee cup. She took off the knit cap and dragged her nails through her flattened hair, almost without thinking.

He watched her with an intense expression.

"There really is nothing else I can add to what I told you already. Let me ask you something. Do you really want to change your situation?"

"You mean, do I want to 'take responsibility for my healing'? That kind of crap?"

"Yes, that kind of crap. Honestly, and I shouldn't be saying this as a therapist. But you seem to revel in your misery."

"Like a pig in slop, yes, Christine," he snapped. "I adore the stink of my life. Just like everyone who lives here adores the stink of the stockyards and the refinery. You get used to it after a while. I'd really miss it if it wasn't here anymore."

"I'll take that for the sarcasm it is. No healthy person would choose to live in this environment."

"Oh, really, Christine. So why'd you come back here? With your degree and smarts you could have gone anywhere. And stayed away for good."

Christine's face gathered itself into something resembling the more professional version of herself. "An opportunity presented itself."

"I never bought that. You crawled back here."

The pose fell away into a hardened version. "Since you're so informed about my career goals, why don't you tell me more, Dr. Thorson. It's your turn."

Arvo swiveled around on his seat, throwing one leg up along the length of the booth. He leaned back and thoughtfully sipped his cold coffee.

"I would say that you're as sick as I am."

"Oh, really. Tell me more."

"While I was skipping school and flunking my classes my senior year, after all the gloried football days were behind me, you were at the top of your game. Class valedictorian. Debate club president. Brilliant and driven it gave you something to do, because at home things weren't such a success."

"I see I'm in the wrong profession." She sounded angry but that was nothing new. "But let me at least suggest something. Abandoned by my father, and I know you are familiar with my history, I sought patriarchal approval through a climb up the ladder. I decided to help others as no one had helped me. Meanwhile, you sought retribution for your lost glory."

"In women and booze. Bravo. You, meanwhile, wandered far from home for a while, but realized that the stink of this place was still with you. You decided to come back and face your demons. Thus, we arrive at the present. You looking like the real you, for once, like you've been dragged through shit. Me pretty much in the same place I've been the past twenty years." He set his cup down.

"Where's the 'and they all lived happily ever after' part?" She had dropped the defenses and sank her head back into the naugahyde, cushioned seatback.

"Well. You know that doesn't ever come true. In our line of work, we see nothing but sad endings."

Arvo reached into his pocket for his phone. "It's Juney."

He flipped open his phone. "How are you, precious?" he asked. "When?" He listened intently. "I'll be there." He snapped the phone shut and jammed it into his pocket.

"I thought you were on leave," Christine said, combing through her hair again with her fingers. "Unless that was just a social call?"

"Are you still seeing Abatha?" he asked, ignoring her question.

"The grandmother called yesterday. She claims Abatha's not feeling well."

"And you believed that?"

"I didn't say anything about believing it. It just opened up my calendar. I don't know when I'll be seeing her again."

"Which explains your availability today, but not so much your wardrobe choice." He held out a napkin to her. "You've got pie on your shirt."

She whipped a Tidestick out of her purse and went to work. He laughed, and she shook her head. "Do me a favor and don't tell anyone you saw me here."

"I'll consider it. Can I ask you a question? A work-related one, I mean?"

"You can ask," she said, scrubbing away.

"What do you make of the case? That is, what's been reported by the sheriff's office and been 'unnamed sourced' into the media."

"Oh, I don't know. That's not really my area," she said, capping the detergent stick and tossing it back into her purse.

"Give it a shot."

She took some time to consider his question. Semis rattled by on the street outside, and a school bus squealed to a stop just outside the restaurant. They'd been sitting for quite a while, Christine observed. A few children stepped off the bus, one a young girl not much younger than Abatha. She watched as the girl stepped in front of the bus to cross the busy street. She waited until she had seen the girl make it all the way across to safety.

Arvo had been watching the little girl too. And watching Christine watch her.

"The story seems premature. In my line of work, I try to ignore too early a diagnosis. Patients report what they think you want to hear, or what they've been telling themselves or others have been telling them about themselves. People that I see tend to be very disconnected from, I guess, their authentic selves."

"So what's your diagnosis about the crime?"

"I'm not buying it."

"Juney isn't either."

"And you, Detective?'

"Three's a crowd, I'd say."

"I'd say. I'm not that happy we have something we agree on." Christine eyed Betty, realizing she hadn't received her tab.

"Something you want?" Betty said. "The coffee's about gone."

"My check?"

"It was paid over an hour ago." Betty tilted her head in Arvo's direction.

"I know, I shouldn't have." Arvo said, pleased. "You can get the next one."

"You know that won't be happening soon."

"Don't count on it. Actually it's coming sooner than you think. Juney heard from one of our informants that some guy has information. On a different dead baby washing up on the river, some years ago. I need to check in on the lead tonight. This is all off the record by the way."

"Is that the related case you mentioned?"

"Sure. It was actually from years ago. Don't you remember?"

Christine had been gathering her things together, but stopped. "Vaguely."

"You were gone then. Maybe that's why the memory is vague. Just over twenty years ago."

"My mother might have mentioned something." Christine remembered her only appointment for the day.

"So are you interested?"

"In what."

"In getting the next tab. See if we can check out this guy's story. After we locate him, of course."

Christine hated to admit it, but she was. "Sure." She needed a better excuse than curiosity. "It's a stretch, but maybe something in this older case might help in treating Abatha."

"Whatever. I'll pick you up at 8:00, tonight. You'll want to clean yourself up a little, not too much. I'm kind of liking the grunge look."

He opened Betty's door and followed her out to the car.

"Are you sure? Might be a rough conversation."

"I can take it. I'll be waiting in my lobby. 8:00."

He watched her drive off, then headed home to clean himself up.

13

CHRISTINE'S MOTHER LIVED ON THE NORTH side of St. Paul, forty-five minutes north of Somerset Hills. Her cramped apartment above a restaurant called the Tin Cup always smelled musty, the walls and floors long steeped in bus and café fumes. And cigarette smoke. Her mother insisted she'd quit smoking years ago, and only occasionally had a cigarette. The stink in the drapery told another story.

Despite her reluctance to have anything to do with Arvo, Christine was glad to have a convenient excuse to shorten the visit with her mother.

"Mother," Christine asked with her head in her mother's refrigerator. "How long has this carton of eggs been in here?"

"Oh, Christine," her mother said in a whiny tone that shredded Christine's nerves, "I don't know. I'm here by myself and you know I don't eat anything. You got them for me."

Yes, Christine thought. *I got them for you like I get everything for you.*

"Why don't you just take them home for yourself? I'll never use them. I don't cook anymore."

When have you ever cooked? Christine thought. She stopped doing anything when Christine's father left her.

She knew her mother took every meal in down at the Tin Cup. The owner sent her the monthly tab. Christine took the eggs out and sniffed the quart of milk. It was only slightly sour and would work fine for the omelets she intended to make for their dinner.

"Why didn't you tell me you'd be coming, Christine? You never let me know when you're coming."

Christine knew this wasn't true but didn't say anything. It was pointless to try and respond to the whining. The clock ticked slower and slower. It was close to 5:00 p.m. and she'd have to stay at least another hour.

Dorla Ivory bustled noisily through the apartment pretending to pick things up, though every time she bent down, she moaned, complaining she'd been on her feet all day and was exhausted, and how inconsiderate it was of Christine to stop by without informing her ahead of time. Christine knew by the stack of crossword puzzle magazines next to her easy chair that her mother had been sitting all day, just like she did every day.

Christine cracked three eggs into a bowl, added milk, and started a skillet heating on the stovetop. She easily navigated her mother's kitchen, after all it had been stocked, outfitted, and maintained by her. She put a few slices of bread into the toaster and set a small counter with two place settings, though she knew she'd be having little. She was still stuffed with pie.

"Mother, come and sit down."

"Christine you know I'm not hungry. I don't know why you bother. It's all going to go to waste."

Christine knew nothing would go to waste. Her mother was complaining about being fussed over. She also complained when she wasn't fussed over. Dorla sat at the counter and lightly primped her permed gray curls, as if she was at the Tin Cup and waiting for a her friend Margie to walk over and meet her for lunch. Christine knew the monthly tab she was sent also included all of Margie's meals.

Christine served her from behind the counter like she was a short-order cook from the café downstairs. She poured a glass of juice for each and joined her mother on one of the two stools. Her mother didn't start eating immediately, her polite way of requesting Christine get up and fetch the salt shaker. She did without comment.

Even though she wasn't hungry, Christine's mother immediately began eating and didn't stop until her plate was clean. Christine cleared the plates and filled the dishwasher while her mother read the *People* magazine Christine had brought with her from the restaurant.

"Mother," Christine asked as she was putting the last of the dishes away. "Do you remember a crime happening, years ago, in Somerset Hills? This would have been when I was in college."

"My memory is not so good anymore," Dorla said, tapping her forehead, moaning a little.

This was also not so, Christine knew, but didn't point it out, for fear of getting her off track. Her mother particularly remembered every injustice she'd experienced, no matter how petty or imagined. She recalled them with little prompting.

"You've seen the news about that baby the girl found, haven't you?" Christine probed.

"Yes. It's terrible. What's wrong with people to throw a human being away like that?" Christine's mother continued reading the *People* magazine as she talked. "That it would happen in that town doesn't surprise me. Nothing has surprised me since your father left. The only good thing about it was that I got myself out of that place as fast as I could."

For Christine's mother, fast meant about a decade after her father left. She hung onto the house even though she couldn't afford it, even with the alimony. Christine was certain her mother thought her father would return, and this kept her going at least for a few years. In fact, the story she told Christine for years was that her father was on an extended company assignment. Even though she was ten when her father left, Christine knew exactly where he was and why he had left. And who he left with.

"Wasn't there a similar case, years ago?"

"Come to think of it," her mother said looking up. "You're right. There was."

"Do you remember anything about it?" Christine asked, wiping the countertop in front of her mother and then hanging the towel to dry on the edge of the sink.

"I'd moved to town by then, hadn't I? Now I remember. I had rented out the house for a while, hoping I could get a good price for it after a few things got repaired. I think it was spring when they discovered that poor baby."

"Can you remember where they found it? Or anything else about what happened?" Christine leaned on the countertop. She knew given enough time the details would come back to her mother. Her memory was perfect.

"Exactly the same place almost, down across from the refinery. I think some kids were down there partying and came across the poor little baby in the wee hours of the morning— yes it was around graduation time, close to the end of the school year. I know that because my sister was congratulating herself for getting your cousin Craig all the way to graduation. Bottom of his class, but he was getting a diploma. Of course I never had that concern with you."

And Christine was sure this fact was pointed out as often as possible to her aunt and cousin. It was no surprise they never spoke to her.

"Did they ever figure out whose baby it was? Who might have been responsible?"

"Not that I know."

Dorla Ivory stood and walked over to her lounge chair. She flicked on the television to catch her favorite quiz show.

"I need to go, Mother," Christine said, collecting her purse.

"You just got here, Christine. You never stay long enough. Why didn't you tell me you weren't going to be here long?"

"I've got something going on tonight."

"A date? You?"

"No mother. It's not a date. And don't act so surprised that it's out of the realm of possibilities."

"So you're leaving and it's not because of a date. Why do you even bother coming up here if you aren't going to stay awhile. You know I'm fine here all by myself, but a little company now and again for me wouldn't hurt you."

Christine walked to where her mother was sitting and kissed her on the forehead. "I'll be back in a few days. I love you, Mother. Say hello to Margie for me."

"Don't forget to take those eggs, Christine. I won't use them." Dorla put the footrest up, turned the television volume up, and returned to her crossword puzzle.

14

CHRISTINE STOOD IN FRONT OF HER CLOSET and for the second time that day, and the second time in her adult life, she had no idea what to wear. She also realized she'd forgotten to ask Arvo where he was taking her, which might have helped her at least narrow down the options. Most likely it was some dive bar, knowing him. Still, it was possible they'd be meeting someone at a more upscale place. In her confused state of mind, more ambiguity didn't help.

She chose a form-fitting Jeremy Laing dress in putty jersey wool, dark hose, and thick black heels. When she felt unsure, she wanted tailoring that displayed her body at its best, she felt the need to arm her beauty for the unknown. It might be the only defense she had, given the unknown destination and person they were meeting. She pulled her hair into a tight ponytail and left her skin bare except for a natural shade of lipstick. She felt confident she'd made the right choice.

She was surprised to hear Arvo ringing for her at the exact time he told her to expect him. She made him wait a few minutes, and then strode through the security door. He glanced at her but said nothing, then turned and walked to his car. Annoyance crept up her spine, though she wasn't sure it was because he said nothing, or because she was bothered that she might actually care what he thought of her.

Arvo's car was cleaner than she'd expected it would be. As he drove away from her fancy condo, they said nothing to each other in the dark. She glanced at his profile lit by the instrument panel. She couldn't tell if his face was actually irritated, or if the blue-cast only suggested it. He had cleaned himself up. She'd noticed he'd shaved, and from what she could see of his clothes, he was dressed decently in a dark pair of gray slacks and a buttoned-down shirt. No tie, but he looked presentable, for once.

They drove along the same road Christine had taken earlier in the day, only this time the scene was modeled only by the available street lighting. In the distance she saw a hazy horizon, lightened from city lights. She still wondered where they were headed, but Arvo seemed in no mood to talk.

They neared the school and the river, neither of which could be seen. The only visible landmark grew larger and larger, gradually blotting out nearly everything. When approached from the ridge of the river bluff, the complex looked like a jeweled crown sitting in a plush velvety valley, the muscular river coursing alongside it with its thick chain of barge traffic. At night, when the river was visually hidden, the refinery bloomed, fed on its raw energy like a fetid night flower. It brilliantly reigned over the landscape for miles around.

They turned on the road that lead to the Rock Island swing bridge and took another immediate right into the parking lot of the King of Spades.

"This is where we're going?" Christine finally spoke up. "You don't expect me to go in there, do you?"

"Suit yourself, Christine. Why I wasted my time coming to get you, I don't know."

He slammed the door behind him and made his way to the door, nodding at the bouncer standing outside. Christine sat for a moment and then got out, scrambling past him. She wondered if any of the clientele might recognize her. She hated to think what she might learn about Somerset Hills. Still, she knew a lot about the dark secrets the residents kept from each other. She realized there was probably nothing this strip club could tell her that she didn't already know.

The bouncer stopped her. "Can I help you?" Unlike Arvo, the bouncer made it completely clear he was aware of what the dress showed off. She stalked around him, knowing he was also well aware of who she was with, someone known and accepted in the club. "Have a nice evening," the man smirked.

Inside, the club pulsated with the blurred intersection of naked skin, burning sound, and raw color and if the refinery had a basement, this was it—the industrial sex and light show—throbbing next to the jugular of one of the most powerful rivers in the world. Spectators leaned on the stage to watch the shimmying flesh and enhanced cleavage of the exotic dancers in various stages of costume. An international variety of spandex, fringed, and sequined cocktail waitresses roamed the floor with trays of drinks high above their heads, but sensibly not blocking anyone's view of the floor show.

Christine at last located the booth where Arvo was, and slid in opposite him.

"I'd say we need to stop meeting at these dives, Christine, but I'm pretty sure you have no intention of keeping this up after tonight. But you owe me a drink, don't you? Or are you going to go all therapeutic on me and not pay for any part of my demise."

Christine kept silent and when the nearly naked waitress arrived, she told her she'd be paying for whatever the gentleman across from her wanted.

"I'd be careful making that kind of offer in a place like this," he said. Arvo finally seemed to be waking up.

Christine ordered a whiskey and soda, a drink much stronger than her usual white wine. The place seemed to demand that. Their orders were quickly delivered, the club after all earned its living from keeping the alcohol flowing. The rest was the base excuse to keep people lingering, a stage show of the carnal and the forbidden.

"When are we seeing what we came to see?"

"You mean the show isn't enough? There is, by the way, a main act. What you see now is only the warm up."

She gave him a disturbed look.

"We'll just have to wait." He leaned back. "And stop looking like a deer in the headlights. That dress is calling more attention to us than I'd like."

The irritation crept up again. He had seen that she could affect others, but not necessarily him. Was that what she wanted? To affect him?

"Just relax. You'll get an education on the finer aspects of life in Somerset Hills. Enjoy the ride."

The drink suddenly warmed Christine up, more than she expected. A second appeared even though she recalled asking for a glass of water, not more whiskey. She pushed the drink towards Arvo, and he pushed it back. "Drink. You need to calm down and blend in to the woodwork here."

A nicely dressed man with a deformed hand came to their table. He reached out to give Arvo a handshake with the bad arm, which had only one finger, the middle one. On it he wore an enormous topaz ring.

"Arvo you're keeping better company these days. Who's your date?"

"Vern Eide, meet Christine Ivory." Christine grasped the proffered finger.

"I'm sorry not to give you a full handshake. I lost the rest of my hand in Bosnia."

Arvo explained. "Peace-keeping mission there in the late '90s. They let him back in the country anyway. He took over this place around then, which frankly was a dump in those days. He cleaned it up nicely, wouldn't you say?"

Arvo motioned Vern to his side of the table and whispered something into his ear. He pointed to the stage.

"The real show's about to begin," Arvo said.

"Enjoy it, pal," Vern said, his hand on Arvo's shoulder. "Miss Ivory, I'm pleased to meet you and hope to see you here again."

"I am *not* your date," Christine corrected him as soon as Eide was out of earshot.

"Christine it's best not to explain what our real association is, hmm? Letting people think we're here for our entertainment, and together, will keep both of us out of trouble. Now, please, sit back. The person we've come to see will be out shortly."

Over the audio system the sounds of a throaty, bluesy sax swelled through the amps from somewhere beneath the thrust stage. The filtered lights switched from blue to a deep purple and went lower and lower until the only thing visible in the darkened room was a dim outline on the stage. An obsidian skinned woman who appeared out of nowhere stood completely still at the center of the stage. She wore a shiny, floor-length dress of dark mesh, and from the bottom of her slender, long legs to her beautiful, perfect breasts—which were clearly unenhanced by cosmetic surgery—she was as smooth as if she had been softly shaped by the gentle erosion from desert sands.

Christine heard the words of *Song of Solomon* in her ears, smelled the myrrh, saw the twin roes, and she knew it was indecent to be thinking the words of the bible in a strip joint, but there was something sacred about this woman's simple, ripe beauty. The sight of this woman's body made her understand what drove men to madness, and she even felt lust riding up inside of her.

The woman on stage moved without moving, transported along by the eyes of the hundred people gathered in the room, her body carried inside their imagination, sinking with them into the depths kept in check deep under the surface during the day. It was night, and this was the safest place to let the carnal roam free.

Like everyone else in the room, Christine forgot why. Why she was in this particular place at this particular time. They were all in the here and now of their deepest forgetting, and that emptied sense just after a confession, all the sins wiped away, the view of pure naked soullessness, relief, the bluesy saxophone hymn rising from the basement and vibrating through the tuning fork of the beautiful African woman on the empty stage. The sacred met the profane, and the lion laid down with the lamb.

At the end of her show, she disappeared even more suddenly then she had appeared as the lights were suddenly cut, and out of respect everyone in the room remained silent for several moments, but then the applause and shouts rose until they were thundering in the room. The stage lights were brought up, and she came out wearing a long silky black robe and bowed as men and women alike tossed money at her.

The two drinks Christine had downed kept her from being able to conceal the awe in her face.

Arvo answered the "who was that" on her face. "That's Mrs. Eide. Vern's wife. She's what kept him going after Bosnia, and what keeps this place going. "

Arvo ordered another drink and arranged for Christine to get her glass of water. The patrons of Spades were returning to some semblance of their pre-Mrs. Eide selves, and the stage remained empty longer in deference to her. Christine sipped at her glass of water, and it gradually dawned on her that they hadn't yet learned anything yet. Not about the case anyway. And what she learned from watching Mrs. Eide couldn't be articulated.

"When are we—" she stopped, noticing that Vern was motioning to Arvo.

"Come on—" Arvo said to her.

"The tab?" Christine said, "unless we're coming back?"

"We're not. And it's already taken care of."

The music was starting to swell for the next dancer, and a few people moved closer to the stage, but it was clear that with Mrs. Eide finished for the moment, the place had lost its core audience. Couples who'd come in for an evening of debauchery were now leaving to pursue more intimate dances in secluded locations. Solo men were drifting around aimlessly, trying their luck with the professionals who'd strategically placed themselves in high traffic areas. One woman wearing a tight sapphire dress was leaning strategically on the bar, her calves accentuated by her six-inch stilettoes. Another sat in a low-cut black dress at a small table in the back, her cleavage on prominent display. She slowly screwed open a lipstick and provocatively pressed its reddened head against her fleshy, moist lips. Another came walking slowly in from the entrance, her short leather skirt slightly askew on her hips, her teased hair loosened from mother-of-pearl combs. She stuffed a wad of bills into a hip pocket, then stopped to shift the skirt into position, smoothing her hands down her hips. Armor in place, she was ready to turn another trick.

Though Christine never liked being dependent, she stuck close to Arvo and felt safer when she saw the fierce looks he was giving the men leering at her. She wondered what line of work they thought she was in and while she wanted to think herself far removed from the business women in Spades conducted, she couldn't help but compare herself to them, these women in the business of hired skin. Was a social worker that far from a prostitute? Both were offering a service intended to relieve suffering, both charged by the hour, required wits, skill, and credentials.

It was where she felt most in control, evaluating and diagnosing other people's problems, and even in the short walk through the crowded strip club, perhaps especially there, the variety of diagnoses she could quickly rattle off matched most of the list in the DSMIV manual code book. From the basic 309.9

Unspecified Adjustment Disorders to 314.01 Predominantly Hyperactive-Impulsive Type of Attention-Deficit/Hyperactivity Disorder; the depressed manic and mixed mood disorders. A quartet of addictions sat together around a table: alcohol, drugs, inhalants, sex—and crossed over into a sojourner on a bar stool. They were all here, enough patients to last her a lifetime and still not cure. Maybe the club was a better place for them and their multiple, complex issues. The club accepted them without question, and the patrons came with clear expectations and got what they wanted. No one was a problem waiting to be solved. Though many doubtless felt themselves beyond repair, here at King of Spades it didn't matter: they weren't here to be repaired, only to forget, for a moment, what it cost them being human.

Vern let them through a small locked door marked "Staff Only" and down a corridor running with racks of skimpy costumes and sound and light equipment boxes and cables. They came to the end of the hallway and descended a small flight of stairs. He opened another door, and they entered a tiny dressing room.

A thin black woman sat in a chair with her back to them, and Vern spoke to her softly. The woman turned and bowed, slightly. It was Mrs. Eide. Christine was surprised to still feel the magnetic pull of her stage presence. Though she seemed smaller in her dressing room, she cast a spell around her that people wore like the sheerest of negligees. Shelves held headdresses on Styrofoam forms, a rack of costumes lined one wall of the room, and a few photographs of young children sat on her dressing table, not even seeming to be out of place. It wasn't surprising that Mr. and Mrs. Eide were supporting a family through the business, but Mrs. Eide seemed too ethereal to have had the time for motherhood.

Vern formally introduced his wife to Christine, but not Arvo. "Mr. Thorson already knows Sarrah. He frequently entertains himself with a visit here." He then excused himself and left the three together.

Christine wondered exactly how much of the club's pleasures Mr. Thorson enjoyed.

"Please," Sarrah Eide said, extending her arm elegantly and gesturing to a pair of folding chairs, "make yourselves comfortable. I wish I could offer you more."

"I—" Christine began, "—your performance . . . was . . . I can't even think of the words to explain."

"You have a new fan, Mrs. Eide. Though I'm sure Ms. Ivory isn't quite sure what to make of her interest in your performance."

Mrs. Eide smiled. "No one ever does. Some find that heightens the experience."

She turned to her mirror and carefully wiped the clear gloss of her lips, and began to braid the long, thick hair that had cascaded freely down her back during the performance. Christine found herself transfixed, then corrected her posture. She was here on professional business and needed to get her head together. She wondered how many drinks she'd actually had.

"I understand you had something to discuss with me," Mrs. Eide asked as her fingers deftly began weaving a complicated five-strand braid close to her skull.

"Yes. Thank you for taking the time to talk to us. We received information in the office that we understand you have some knowledge about."

"Please, ask whatever you wish." Christine couldn't place the African accent in Sarrah's speech. It was another intoxicating mystery of Sarrah's. Even though Christine wished she could look away and focus on exactly what Arvo was asking—she really did need to concentrate for Abatha's sake—she was lost in the sight of the graceful, black fingers appearing and disappearing into the dark, flowing river of hair and the exotic voice. She forced herself to turn and watch Arvo instead, who was leaning on a dressing table next to her. She shielded her eyes from the wondrous secrets Sarrah Eide wove into her hair.

"What does the word Mississippiboi mean to you?"

"It's a name, Detective."

"A name. Can you tell me more? What makes you think of it as a name?"

Mrs. Eide continued the slow, purposeful, experienced weaving of her hair. "As you are well aware, Detective, the club has a number of regulars."

"Yes, I am well aware of that."

"We also have, how shall I say, a number of people who come here to conduct various personal business." Sarrah wrapped a band around one of her braids. "We know that our customers appreciate our discretion, especially when it comes to how people finance the pleasures they find here."

"I know that you want to keep the special reputation this club has for confidentiality, but for Ms. Ivory's sake, could you explain?"

"My husband in his line of work must keep his tax records and receipts organized. I help him with the bookkeeping. To assure our clientele that the club remains a private haven, we offer accounts to some of our favorite customers."

"And no, Christine, so you don't need to worry about protecting your professional reputation, I do not keep an account here. Though I've been offered an even more private arrangement by my good friends, the Eides."

"And that offer remains open." Mrs. Eide had finally secured the end of her long, remarkable weaving.

"Please go on, we weren't talking about my non-existent—" he emphasized for Christine "—account."

"Yes. We offer some private, identity-masked accounts for our best customers. The name Mississippiboi is associated with one of the accounts."

Christine thought she'd attempt a remark. "Doesn't sharing this information with us jeopardize the club's reputation?"

"Ms. Ivory. For some we make very strategic deviations. Detective Thorson is one of those people."

"So, to be perfectly clear, you have an account with the name 'Mississippiboi,' who we could safely assume is a regular here." Arvo shot Christine a look that suggested he wished he hadn't invited her.

"He is a regular, though for the past several months, he seems to have had less time for us. One of his personal business associates here mentioned he'd been traveling frequently in the past several months." Mrs. Eide got up from her chair and walked to a file drawer in another corner of the tiny room. She pulled a ledger book out.

"Yes, there was a slight break in his patronage over the summer. He returned here for my most recent show in the past few weeks. Since then, we've seen him every day or so. Though he wasn't in the audience tonight."

"So you would recognize him if you saw him."

"Of course. I could point him out to you. My obligations to the club though do not permit me to tell you his real name. That of course is what they pay you for, in your line of work."

Though at the moment, Arvo's line of work was on mandatory leave.

"Does the staff know what Mississippiboi's line of work is?"

"I believe it may be connected to the government, though again, I can't say more."

"Because you don't know or because discretion is required."

"These types of associations can harm us more than the customer, though it might be difficult for anyone to believe. There are certain kinds of light we don't want shined too brightly on the club. The harsh spotlight of the media would shut down many sources of revenue to us."

"I understand that very well, Mrs. Eide."

"I have to prepare for my next performance, so I hope you have no further questions at this time."

"Only that if you would be so kind as to let me know when you next see Mississippiboi in the audience, I would be very appreciative."

"Mr. Eide and I are happy to inform you, if we know that whatever further conversations you may have with the gentleman take place at some distance from this establishment."

"You know you can trust me," Arvo said.

Vern returned to escort Arvo and Christine back upstairs to the busy club. Crowds were once again gathering. Everyone knew that Mrs. Eide performed twice, and they knew exactly when to be ready for it.

Christine looked at Arvo. "Please. Can we go somewhere else?" A second show would be too much for her over-stimulated senses.

Without a word he walked her to his car and they drove away as more cars filled the parking lot and people—wounded, remorseful, or otherwise burdened—scurried past the bouncer and into the redeeming darkness of the club.

15

ARVO DROVE CHRISTINE AWAY from the King of Spades along the dark and deserted River Road. The clock on his dash was broken, but Christine knew it must be past 1:00 a.m. The refinery was behind them, still lighting the sky and blotting out any view of the stars. A wan quarter moon hung limply above the western horizon like a small child dragging behind its distant mother.

They drove in silence for a while, heading south in the direction of Christine's condo. Christine watched Arvo out of the corner of her eye. She could see him nervously glancing in the rear-view mirror. She turned to look out her window.

Suddenly he sped up, taking a sharp curve fast and throwing Christine against her door. He took another sharp curve and she was thrown the opposite way, her arms jerking wildly and her left hand ending up on Arvo's lap.

"Well, now we're getting somewhere," he said.

She snatched her hand away. "Is it really necessary to drive this fast?" she snapped, still feeling dizzy from the effects of alcohol and the club. The jarring turns were making her feel nauseous.

Arvo didn't answer, but she noticed him still glancing frequently in the rear-view mirror. She looked in the side mirror. She could see the headlights of another car a short distance behind them, keeping pace with Arvo's.

"Are we being followed or something?"

"That's what I'm trying to figure out."

"What, by drag racing in the dark?"

Arvo took another fast turn, and Christine could see the car still behind them, the same distance it had been, obviously matching Arvo's pace. He turned and drove up a gravel road, his tires spinning and spitting gravel as they skidded across the slippery surface. Christine watched as the car behind them took the same turn.

"Does that answer your question?" Arvo said, making another hard curve to turn onto the county road.

Arvo jammed the gas pedal down and squealed east on the county road, heading across a pitch black plain. Here the road went straight for miles, poorly lit at intersections with a few, scattered farm roads. The car behind them continued its pursuit. Christine glanced nervously at the speedometer, watching the needle creep up, beyond, and then far beyond the speed limit.

She noticed they were closing in on a railroad crossing a short distance ahead.

They sped across, and the pursuing car followed soon after. The faint sound of the horn of an approaching train could be heard somewhere south. Christine looked in the rear view mirror to see the lights of the warning arm flashing behind them.

"Great." Arvo said, gunning his motor, the smell of burning rubber making Christine feel even more sick.

"I think I'm going to throw up," Christine said.

"Hold on," Arvo said.

"I'm not sure—"

"I meant—brace yourself," he shouted.

The car behind them kept closing in when suddenly Arvo jammed on the brakes, spinning the car around and into the wrong lane. The car chasing them was now coming directly at them. It swerved off the road just narrowly avoiding crashing into Arvo and Christine head on. Arvo again hit the gas and sped back towards the railroad tracks.

Ahead the crossing arms were blinking red and just swinging down, and the train itself was less than a half-mile from the intersection, speeding across the deserted countryside with its horn warning it was near the crossing.

"Shit," Christine said. "You aren't going to—"

"Hang on," Arvo snarled. He came to the track, and immediately jerked his steering wheel to the right, sending the car banging hard against the raw rails as they began to pass over. Out Christine's window, she could see the train engine and clearly make out the red-faced engineer, his mouth forming an expletive.

Suddenly they were on the other side and the train was barreling past, its horns still blasting. Arvo quickly drove up onto the county road and sped off as Christine turned to watch the train.

"How much time do we have?" Arvo said.

"I can't tell—it's too dark to see how long the train is."

They raced back to the east, turning north when they came to the river again. Arvo flew into the King of Spades lot, parked, and killed his lights.

"Come on," he said, jumping out of the driver's side, and running the car around to yank Christine out.

"Stop it, Arvo!" she said.

"God damn it, Christine. We've got thirty seconds at most." He held her hand and almost dragged her past the bouncers and back into the club. He quickly ushered her around the stage and into one of the secluded booths at the far end of the stage. Arvo kept watch on the entrance, and Christine followed his eyes. Two big men in dark suits entered.

Arvo suddenly drew his arms around Christine, pulling her to him, his mouth against hers. "Fake it," he ordered into her mouth. She could feel the hard metal of his gun jamming against her. She felt his hand on the back of her head. The other she could feel sliding down between them to his weapon, which he carefully slid out of the holster.

"Keep it up," his mouth moving around to her ear, "Don't stop until I tell you."

Christine stayed where she was and felt Arvo's hot lips on her neck, the side of her face, and back on her mouth. Her heart pounded, and she felt dizzy and warm, almost as if she were melting. In her hazy confusion, she was trying to sort out why she was feeling what she was. Was it some combination of the chase and the booze? She was sure she couldn't be feeling anything for this man who seemed bent on disgusting and using her. Yet his ardor felt so real.

At last Arvo snapped away from her. He pushed her into the corner of the booth and made a wide survey of the club, his eyes finally catching Vern's. Vern walked over.

"Who were those guys who followed us in here?" Arvo said.

"They were after you?" Vern said. "I've never seen them before tonight. They came in earlier, I was afraid they were IRS snoops."

"They were here earlier?"

"Yeah. I think they left a half-hour ago."

"Right after we left."

Vern glanced in the direction of one of his bouncers, a tough man with a Marine style haircut that Arvo knew. Vern waved the man over and exchanged a few words with him, then sent him off to the entrance. "James will keep an eye out until we're sure those two guys are gone for good."

"Thanks, Vern."

"I usually don't mess with your business, Arvo, but what do you think those guys were following you for? I mean, federal guys? Aren't you all on the same side?"

"That's what you'd think, but that's not always the case."

"You know I welcome you here, Arvo, but for the sake of the rest of my customers, I have to make sure we don't see them around here again. I know you understand, Arvo. Nothing personal."

Arvo shrugged his shoulders.

"I'll send a girl over with some refreshments for you. James will stop by with an 'all clear' for you later."

Christine thought she should ignore the drink quickly placed in front of her, but had it anyway, even though it barely impacted her nervous state. After waiting for another half-hour, James nodded at Arvo and they finally left the club.

Arvo stood next to Christine's side of the car, opening the door gallantly as she approached. "Madam?" he said. She got in, slamming herself into the seat.

He noticed Christine inspecting her knee, which was bleeding slightly.

"When did that happen?"

"Hard to tell—between being chased by some goons halfway across the county, dragged into a strip club, and forcibly assaulted, by you no less. I haven't really had time to notice until now."

"Assaulted? Right." He reached over her to the glove compartment, saying "Excuse me," as he hit the latch. A couple of receipts tumbled out as he dug around inside it to retrieve a first aid kit.

"Here," he said, opening the kit and retrieving a packet of antiseptic and a bandage.

"Thanks, really. You've been so helpful."

"Look, I had no idea the evening was going to turn out this way."

"Right. Like I've really enjoyed this night, Arvo."

"You know you wanted to be here."

"What, you mean in that dark booth just now. At the club? I did not want that."

"That's the first thing that came to your mind?"

Christine's eyes snapped on Arvo's face.

"Look, Christine. I didn't exactly plan that."

Her brows went up.

"No. I didn't. I know you want to know the truth about who killed that baby, maybe not for the baby's sake, but for Abatha. I know it and you know it."

"It's not very clear what tonight had to do with any of that," she said, still dabbing her knee.

He started the engine and they pulled onto the road. "It may have everything to do with Abatha. Juney said some government guy is sniffing around about the older case. Had heard the guy might be a customer of the Eides. Before you can make a connection, you need the dotted line. We may or may not have two dots in our line, depending upon whether this Mississippiboi is the same person checking in about the baby that died years back."

"We don't even know whether the two cases are connected." Christine said.

"No, we don't. Look, I'm sorry you tore open your knee. I'm sorry you were forced to endure such proximity to me. If you want, I won't involve you in any more of this. Just say the word."

"Damn it I can't see what I'm doing," Christine said. She opened the glove box to use its interior light on her knee. She ripped open a bandage and put it on. When she finished, she began to pick up the clutter that had fallen out of the glove compartment.

"Apologies? I'm sorry I shouldn't be looking at these. I can't help reading things that are right in front of my face." Christine could clearly see who was being apologized to and whom was apologizing.

She quickly shoved all the papers back into the glove box and attempted to slam it shut, several times, but it kept popping open.

"Forget about it, just leave it alone. Look, I know it's late, let's go get a cup of coffee. See if it helps calm our nerves." He took a handful of the apologies and tossed them, with the first aid kit, into the back seat.

Christine sighed and agreed. Arvo turned off River Road onto the highway, and they headed towards the city, both wanting to put a good distance between themselves and everything that happened under the bright, raucous spotlights of the King of Spades.

16

ARVO FOUND A PLACE TO PARK along St. Peter, a boulevard filled with upscale restaurants and shops, near a park in the center of town. They got out and walked in the chilly air, looking for any place that might be open late. Even in this part of town, a few street walkers were strutting around advertising their availability, hoping to snare a rich banker or real estate developer. A trick like that could bring in enough money to last a girl a good long time, unless she blew it right away buying crack up on Cathedral Hill.

Neon lights blinked LIVE JAZZ NIGHTLY over a small door. Arvo didn't ask Christine whether she liked jazz, it appeared to be one of the only places open. They ducked inside. A melodious cascade of chords and notes rose from a lower floor, and following the quiet melody of a Thelonious Monk's "Ruby My Dear," they descended gratefully, sinking into a small couch somewhere in the back of the sparsely filled room.

A couple nursing the dredges of amber-filled glasses eyed them as they sat down.

A small round table in front of them showed evidence of the previous occupants. A lipstick stained glass, numerous watery rings on the table, a single ticket stub from a concert at the orchestra hall around the corner. Maybe a streetwalker had earned her week's pay with the combination of the right words, tease, and worked some poor guys lust into a horniness he was willing to shell out a couple of hundred to ease. Everyone had something to sell.

"Coffee? Or something else?"

"I don't know."

This left it to Arvo to decide. He ordered two brandies, warmed. The waiter wiped off their table and relit the candle that had flickered out. He returned shortly with their brandies, and then went back to his station: the bar next to the band.

The quartet—the pianist, a sax player, bassist, and drummer, smoothly moved into their next number, which was sultrier than either Arvo's or Christine's mood wanted, posing questions neither was ready to answer. Arvo swirled a brandy glass above the candle, then handed it to Christine.

"It will take the edge off."

Christine sipped the warm liquid and felt it melt down her throat. She realized as she felt the slow burn in the back of her throat and the spreading warmth through her limbs how exhausted she was. This was the drink after the last drink she should have had.

"I need to tell you something," she said, a bit woozy from all the alcohol. "I don't like how you treat me . . . with such contempt. I know we have a different approach to work, and I totally disagree with yours. But I will say this, knowing I might regret it later. Your heart is in the right place. The rest is in the gutter."

"Oh," Arvo said. "You actually do have a soft spot for me. Maybe that kiss put you over the top."

Christine glared at him through her blurry eyes. "That had nothing to do with it. I just felt the need to be honest. But I will say one more thing."

"What's that?"

"Don't ever grab me like that again . . . I don't care if we're being chased down by Satan himself."

"I will do whatever is necessary. I'm sorry there wasn't time to ask your frickin' permission first. And just for the record, it was a defensive move."

Christine laughed. "Defensive? I'd hardly call it that. It was an aggressive move. You took advantage of the situation."

"Are you trying to suggest there's more to it than that?"

"Yes," she said boldly, encouraged by the brandy. She attempted to gracefully pose herself on the couch. "I happen to know, and many concur, that I am an attractive woman." Attractive, but barely able to keep a sober expression on her face after the excessive quantity of liquor she'd drunk that night.

"Yes, you're attractive, there's no question. But I need to explain something to you, though I wonder how much of this conversation you'll remember tomorrow." He reached for her brandy glass. "Maybe I should have gone with the coffee."

She pulled it away. "No way, Detective Thorson. You will not be relieving me of my warm brandy, not anytime soon." She held up her glass in the waiter's direction, and he brought her a refill. She attempted to swirl it over the candle as she'd seen Arvo do, but held it too close and for too long. "Ouch!" she shrieked, pulling her hand away from the candle.

Arvo caught the glass just in time and set it on the table. He quietly motioned for the tab.

"Oh," she said examining the side of her hand. "It's just a flesh wound. I'll be good as new by morning. Which reminds me, you were telling me shomething you'd like me to remember in the morning?"

"It's hardly worth it to bring it up at the point."

"I inshist . . . I inshist you tell me whatever is on your mind."

"To satisfy your morbid curiosity I will tell you something. Yes, Christine Ivory. You are an attractive woman. Maybe on the high maintenance side, but still attractive. To spare your feelings about certain things that happened tonight, I want you to understand that it meant absolutely nothing to me, but not because you aren't attractive, because you certainly are."

He took another look at her and saw she seemed to be concentrating on what he was saying. He continued to swirl the brandy over the flame. He cleared his throat, and sat remembering better times. A small smile passed over his face, and then his expression quickly turned sad. Focusing on the flame, he continued.

"I'll admit something to you that no one else knows," he said quietly, his voice just starting to crack. "I am still in love with my wife."

He cleared his throat again and cupped the warm glass. "I know. I should have said ex-wife."

"As stupid as that sounds, even to me, it's the truth. I'm not over her. I'm not sure I'll ever get over that woman even though she cheated on me constantly and dumped me, and obviously never thinks about me except when she's waiting for me to send her money. I guess that may make me a high-maintenance kind of guy, you and I at least have that in common."

Arvo made the longest, most honest disclosure he'd ever made to anyone. He replayed it in his mind, cross-examining himself on the level of his honesty. Was it true that he still loved Helen? Or was he simply in denial, reeling from the hurt of being loved, then lied to, and then rejected. He continued to stare into the candle with Christine's glass in his hand. Maybe Christine could sort it all out for him. He steeled himself to look at her face and see her reaction, which might tell him how much of an idiot he was. And whether it was possible to be healed. He turned to see her-curled up against a pillow she'd made of his jacket, deep asleep.

Arvo handed the waiter a couple of twenties for the brandies and thanked him. He put an arm under Christine's shoulder and got her to her feet, half-carrying her up the stairs to his car. She seemed barely aware she was being moved. When he got her into her side of the car, she quickly fell deeply asleep. He noticed what appeared to be familiar car lights on him a short way away, and then realized he was seeing things. It was only a cab.

In the silence of his car, he thought more about his ex-wife, and it dawned on him that he was having trouble remembering her face clearly. He'd seen her infrequently over the past year, and even less over the past few months. Fragments of her were slipping away. One thing he thought he'd never forget was her smell: a combination of honey musk and smoky bourbon. He realized, just then, that part of her smell might have come from the men she saw. The men she slept with while still married to Arvo.

He was dumbfounded. Of course. How could he have been so blind to neglect that detail? And, just now, he thought sadly how he missed that particular smell. Of Helen. When all along what he was remembering, so vividly, was the smell of other men on her. The thought of it made the memory turn bitter. He forced himself to concentrate on something else.

He noticed that Christine was wearing a completely different fragrance, one he couldn't place. So much close contact with her seemed to leave her smell all over him. He put his hand to his nose, the hand that he'd cupped against her head when he pulled her face to his and kissed her so hard and so long that even his lips felt rubbed raw. He inhaled slowly and deeply the smell of a different woman, hoping it would wipe Helen completely away. There it was—the scent of Christine: clean, crisp citrus and a trace of something he couldn't place. A fresh light floral, the smell of a simple garden flower. The rest of the drive, he kept the hand close to his face, inhaling Christine and exhaling Helen, trying hard to exorcise the sick love from his system, though there really wasn't yet a new healthy one to replace it.

He checked on Christine in the rear view mirror. She was still peacefully slumbering in his back seat. He shook his head. No one at the department would ever believe that proper, stiff and yes, sexy as hell Christine Ivory was passed out drunk in his back seat. And that he'd gotten a good, passionate kiss out of her, a kiss that she actually seemed to enjoy. A kiss that maybe he too had enjoyed, at least slightly.

17

ARVO NOTICED THE WEATHER had turned colder over the weekend, a cold front must have come through. The skies were overcast in lumpy inedible gravy gray, as if the clouds were putting on weight for a long winter ahead. Soon Arvo would have to keep the car idling during his time in front of the Eagle's Club.

He'd dropped Christine at her place early Saturday morning and spent the rest of the weekend in his apartment, not exactly exhausted and not exactly in a state of shock, but somewhere in between. Numb. Not an unusual state of mind for him, but he felt a small difference that was even more noticeable this morning. A strange sensation in his hands. He wondered at first if arthritis was coming on, it ran in his family. But he knew enough about it to expect that the strange tingling sensation in his hands felt more like what he remembered from an experience with frostbite. More a painful thawing out than a freezing up. He wasn't thawing out from an actual case of frost-bite, that wasn't possible. But some other unnamed feeling was coming back into him. He wasn't sure he liked it.

Since he hadn't left his apartment, he hadn't been in his car since predawn Saturday. When he cut his engine at the Eagle's Club he sat back, and after gazing across the street to the shabby building and its skimpy boulevard hackberry tree, he prepared for the second ritual. Then he remembered. The apologies were scattered all over the passenger side, on the seat, on the floor, fallen like leaves from a tree. He unbuckled his seat belt and reached over to gather the ones on the floor. He left small piles of them on the seat, also picking up the small packet containing the used antiseptic pad. A couple of apologies had been bled on. Christine had managed to leave an impression on his car, to say the least. Arvo found himself chuckling at the small splotches of blood wiped across one memorable apology, written on the back of a hotel receipt where Helen had met one of her lovers.

The chuckling caught Arvo by surprise. He sighed and looked at the rearview mirror, wondering what to think of himself, then he noticed the rest of the apologies randomly located in the back seat. He couldn't quite remember how they'd gotten there. He wedged himself awkwardly between the driver and passenger buckets of the Ford and reached into the back seat to retrieve the bits of apologies that had landed there.

Finally, the accumulated pile was together in one place on the passenger side. He began to take each apology and press them flat between his tingling hands. He was not reading them as deeply as usual, trying to make sense of the sincere, but completely illusory words in front of him. He knew Helen had meant every word of what was written on the scraps of paper in front of him, but she never kept any of the promises written on these little pieces meant for the trash. Arvo knew he never believed a word she said. Still, he kept every slip of paper.

He stacked up the apologies and squeezed the whole wad back in place in his glove compartment. He retrieved the first-aid kit tossed in the back seat as well, straightened out the supplies, and wedged it back as well.

Thorson rubbed his hands together, trying to massage the tingling out. He almost didn't feel the phone vibrating urgently in his pocket.

It was Juney texting him. "Turn on your TV." Television he did not yet have installed in his car, and he was surprised Juney assumed he was in a comfortable easy chair at home, she knew the morning ritual, and should have suspected he kept it up, even with the caveat that he was out on leave.

He switched on the radio in time to hit a few seconds in to the top of the hour news brief. He heard something about the coroner's report, and a press conference scheduled later in the day. He hit the redial to call Juney as the reporter stated that while the communications officer speaking on record wouldn't release any additional information, sources inside the government center were saying that the report was inconsistent with the existing direction the investigation was taking.

"Juney, you know what I'm looking for," he said almost before she answered. "And . . ." he said quashing her objection, already coming through over the phone. "I don't want to hear you say you can't, because you always come through anyway. Lunch is on me at Betty's."

"Including the uh . . . manicure?"

"A manicure, eh? Since when are you fussy about your nails? I get it, there are people around. Are we on?"

"Yes," she said. "I'm glad you could fit me in on such short notice at the salon."

Arvo smiled to no one. "Yes, we'll do that purple spike Mohawk, just like you requested."

"Thank you, Betty. I'll see you at noon then."

"I'll be wearing the shower cap and the blow torch. See you then." He hung up.

He glanced at his watch and saw there was just enough time to visit the boss before lunch.

When Arvo arrived at the county building a few reporters were still hanging out in the lobby. One recognized him and started walking his way, but Arvo passed him and slid into an open elevator. The elevator stopped at the mezzanine level. Christine got on with a cup of coffee from the cafeteria.

"Don't look so annoyed. I'm not going to bite you. Or do anything else." He winked.

Christine moved to the opposite corner. "I'm just surprised to see you here. Is the leave over?"

"No. Did you hear the news this morning? Coroner's report just came in. I'm going to demand to see it."

They arrived at Christine's floor. Arvo had forgotten to hit the floor he needed. He got out with her.

"Look," she said stopping in the hallway. "I know I may have said some things Friday night, but I thought about this long and hard over the weekend."

"About what, exactly?" he almost smirked.

"The investigation. Keep me out of it from here on out. It isn't my area and being involved with you, even for semi-professional reasons, is not a good idea."

"I guess a second date, or it would be a third if you count the lunch we had, is out of the question then?"

A couple of paralegals exited another elevator and came walking past Christine and Arvo. He stepped out of the way to let them through, requiring him to come closer to Christine. Once they had passed, she began to stalk off, mumbling quietly, "And please, don't bother my patients, either."

He watched her walk away, admiring the line of her tailored wool pants. "By the way, I haven't quite got all your blood stains out of my upholstery," he said right when Christine came to her office door.

She reached for the door knob and banged her hand clumsily on it in her hurry to get away. The jarring movement caused her to juggle her coffee cup, sloshing coffee onto the floor and dribbling some on her hand. She grabbed for the door handle again, growing angrier as it slipped in her wet hand. Once she did make it inside, she slammed the door.

"I'll send you the detailing bill," he shouted, turning to the elevator bank.

Arvo entered the sheriff's office suite without announcing himself, except to nod at the lovestruck receptionist, who on seeing him began to smooth her hair and blush.

"Bill," he said entering the sheriff's office without knocking.

"—Arvo, how's the leave going? Just stopping by on a social call? HR have your leave processing correctly?"

"I'm not here on a social call. I heard the autopsy report is out. I came to see it." Arvo commandeered a chair by the wall and dragged it over to Ruud's desk. He sat with a look that said he expected the report.

"Now, Arvo. What's this about? You're on leave. This isn't something you need to be involved with. The case has been reassigned."

"Bill. I don't leave things unfinished and you know that. The report must have made its way to your office by now."

"As a matter of fact, it hasn't." Bill reshuffled some papers on his desk.

"If you're saying that it procedurally isn't here, I understand how the procedures work. I don't care if it hasn't 'officially' arrived in the office yet. I know you get an advance unofficial copy. Let me see that one and I'll be on my way."

"I'm sorry. That won't be possible. And I'll say this again. You are on leave. Go act like it. Don't make things more difficult than they already are."

Bill got up and walked to the door of his office, opening it and looking back at Arvo.

"I mean it Arvo. I know you don't like what's happening to you, but I'll ask you for me. For my reputation. Please, leave."

Arvo waited where he was, but soon saw by the look on the sheriff's face it was pointless. He headed to the door.

"Please, Arvo. Don't show your face around here, not until the end of your leave. You need a doctor's permission to return to work. I'm not telling you that because some procedure demands I do that. I tell you that as a friend."

"And I will tell you, I don't need your help, even as a friend." Arvo left without looking back. The clerk pouted after him.

He had asked, he told himself as he rode the elevator down. He had done things according to the damned procedures everyone insisted on. He'd been rejected and turned away. Now he would do things his way.

Juney was waiting for him at Betty's, and he told the waitress to give her whatever she wanted. He wasn't hungry, though he snitched a few of her fries. His procedure called for timing and attention to certain details, like making sure your inside source was well fed.

The plates were taken away, a fresh cup of coffee placed in front of her, and the bill was paid with only pleasantries exchanged up to that point. Juney lit up her after-lunch cigarette, telling Arvo it was time for her to talk.

"The baby's been dead for months," Juney told him. "The girl they took in is being processed to be released."

"You saw the report?"

"You had to ask? What do you think?" she asked, in mock offense.

Juney had a friend in the coroner's department. The friend had access to the official report, but only for minutes, so that meant Juney made her way to an empty office in the coroner's department where the report would be left, in an unmarked folder, for the few minutes Juney needed to devour every detail. On cue, a few minutes after Juney left the office, the friend returned, and refilled the report in the official location. No one was the wiser. The friend was handsomely rewarded with a batch of Juney's secret recipe fudge.

Juney didn't need a photocopy to recall the exact details later. She had made a mental snapshot as good as any by a high-powered, mega-pixel camera. As she recounted what she read to Arvo, he saw her look up, her eyes moving back and forth, as if she were reading from a sheet stowed in some file cabinet of her brain.

Juney related all the details, though they were gruesome, the level of minutiae made it sound more clinical, than tragic. This didn't mean that Juney had no compassion: she had more than she could handle at times, and given her job and her amazing memory, there was much to be compassionate about. Today, however, she knew what Arvo wanted, and that she delivered: the findings made by the coroner as to the probable cause of death, whether the baby had died before, or after, going into the water. Judging by the status of the lungs and contents of the stomach, and other forensic determinations, the baby had been born alive and had been alive in the moments before its drowning. DNA profiling was underway. There was nothing she would forget from her once-only reading of the corners report. This they both knew.

"So that's everything? Baby was alive at birth, apparently healthy, and it's clear the baby died from drowning. Likely been in the water for a few months at the least."

Juney nodded. "That's everything. Oh. Wait."

Arvo waited. For some reason, Juney had withheld a final detail.

" It was a girl."

They paused for a moment. A perfectly healthy baby girl, someone's daughter or granddaughter. Tossed out like a piece of garbage. Juney looked at Arvo and saw the hardened look in his eye.

"Now that's everything."

"You're sure. Everything."

"Since when do you question me?" She picked at her teeth with a toothpick.

"I think for once you missed something, though I can't believe it myself. Maybe you're the one needing a leave." He leaned on his hand, smiling a little to throw her off. He didn't want to challenge her too much. Even he was stunned that she seemed to have left out an important detail.

"What are you talking about? And how would you even know if I missed something."

"Come on. Okay, maybe you're kidding me or something. Maybe it was removed before the coroner saw her, though I think that would be against procedure."

Juney gave him a blank, somewhat miffed look.

"The bracelet? Silver beaded bracelet on her arm?"

"What are you talking about?" She looked confused. "Are you joking with me? Kind of lame. A bracelet?"

He looked at her without smiling this time.

"There was no bracelet. I am not kidding and I did not forget anything and no, nothing would have been removed before the coroner started in. You know as well as I do how these things work."

Arvo's face began to go pale. He felt the color start to drain out of him.

"Something's not adding up here, is it?" Juney said.

"The girl, Abatha, she mentioned a bracelet. She was very specific about it. It's too odd a detail for a kid to just make up on the spot. Especially a kid like this one."

"Arvo. I told you. There was nothing about a bracelet. I think you need to talk to that girl again."

"I think I do, too." He got up, in a hurry, knocking a menu tent onto the floor. Betty looked over. "I got it, sorry Betty."

"Arvo." Juney had one last thing to tell him.

"I know. It's all off the record. You don't have to worry."

"Look, I know you know that. Is there something you want me to do about this bracelet?" Juney's face was knotted in concern. "I mean, potentially, we have an evidence problem here."

Arvo knew she took her job very seriously. She could be held responsible for missing evidence and now she could be implicated, just by virtue of Arvo mentioning the witness's interview. But Arvo knew that what she was most concerned about was the very idea of someone, somehow, tampering with an investigation.

"Potentially is the right word. We don't know anything for certain right now, and I don't want you to do anything about it now. Just keep your eyes and ears open. And let me know, right away, if anything comes to light."

She nodded. Her face relaxed. "You're the boss, right?"

He smiled, placing a hand on her shoulder. "Yes, I'm the boss. And it's going to be okay."

She smiled. "Thanks for lunch, boss."

"Let's do it again, real soon," Arvo said, racing out the door.

18

ARVO DROVE TOO FAST through the hilly back roads, knowing very well it wasn't a good idea. He remembered the exact spots where auto accidents over the past twenty or thirty years claimed the lives of the reckless. But he had no choice, he had a bad feeling about the girl and he needed to see Christine, and before the press conference. He needed to find a way to talk to Abatha. She was the only link between the killer and the truth, and he suspected he wasn't the only one who knew that.

He squealed into the county building parking lot and ran into the building at 4:00 p.m. The press conference would be at 6:00. There might enough time to get to Abatha, but it would have to be in a way that wasn't going to raise an alarm, alerting the media and potentially, the killer. He would have to involve Christine, who he knew wanted nothing to do with him.

The elevators weren't cooperating either. Many of the county employees were leaving work by 4:00 p.m., so all of the elevators would be running slowly down from the upper floors, stopping at every floor, and jammed with employees eager to get out of the building and head home. He impatiently drummed his finger on the UP button at the ground floor. He knew very well this hurried nothing. Finally one of the elevators arrived and he pushed his way in past the exiting employees, pounding the DOOR CLOSED button. The door closed and he went straight to the sixth floor.

He ran down the hall and nearly ripped Christine's office door off its hinges. She was with a whimpering elderly woman and both looked at him—the elderly woman like she was having a heart attack and Christine like she was about to kill him.

"Arvo Thorson, I'm calling security. Get out!" Christine commanded, standing up to come and push him out of the room, if it was necessary.

Arvo was panting. "Abatha . . . need to talk to her . . ." He put his hands on his knees. He was really out of shape, winded just from running down the hall.

"Arvo, I said I am done with my involvement in this mess of yours. And I am with a patient. What do you think by barging in here?"

"Just . . . Listen! The girl might be in serious danger." He leaned against her wall. He was seriously in need of more exercise and less booze.

That got Christine's attention. "Wait outside, Arvo. Please. We're nearly finished here."

Christine sent him out into the hallway and Arvo paced, for what seemed like half an hour but he knew was only a few minutes. Finally Christine's door opened and the elderly woman shuffled out, giving Arvo a wide berth and watching him closely, as if she feared him pouncing on her at any moment.

She ushered him into her office and closed the door. She didn't bother to offer him a chair, or sit down herself.

"What is going on?"

"The baby's been dead a while . . . not hers." Arvo could hardly breathe.

"What?" Christine said upset and confused.

"The autopsy report came out, press conference tonight. That girl they arrested . . . released."

"Wait a minute. It can't be hers? I don't understand what you're saying."

Arvo finally sat down. He gave his breathing a chance to catch up. "The immigrant has been ruled out as the mother of the dead baby. This woman they hauled in has nothing to do with the case. Meaning the real culprit is still out there. And there's more."

"I still don't get what this has to do with Abatha."

"The bracelet. The baby's bracelet. It wasn't mentioned in the report. The autopsy."

"So it wasn't mentioned. So what."

"Don't you get it? Do you believe what Abatha said during the interview? Do you think she was making anything up? Or forgetting anything?"

Christine thought about Abatha. She had spoken so rarely, so there was little to base an important opinion on. Christine went through her memory of the therapy sessions and replayed Arvo's interview with her. The detailed descriptions of the animals, the birds, the weather, the intricate knowledge of the road along the river, and then that horror of the discovery. Even at the most difficult moments of the interview, with tears running down her face, the girl's voice was steady, and her observations precise.

Arvo was watching Christine's face as she recalled every interaction with the girl. Soon he saw her recognition of exactly was at stake, spreading its alarm across her face.

"She wouldn't forget anything." Christine's eyes got larger. "That girl would not make anything up."

"Exactly."

"I still don't quite . . ." Christine tried hard to picture how the news would affect Abatha.

"Someone is tampering with the investigation. And the evidence. Something is being covered up."

"If what you are saying is true—if someone is trying to hide what really happened, then . . . what does this mean about a witness with knowledge of evidence, now missing . . ."

"—That might point in a direction of the real suspect? When the suspect, or an accomplice, has tried so obviously to point elsewhere? Including, possibly, by tipping the police along some false direction?"

The full force of the implications hit Christine. She ran to her desk and grabbed her purse, ransacking it. "Where the hell is my Blackberry?" She dumped it onto her desktop, finally revealing the Blackberry at the bottom of the pile.

Arvo watched as Christine's hands shook. Her fingers worked furiously through to some bit of information. "That's it." She hit a button and put the phone on speaker.

A woman answered.

"Margaret, it's me, Christine Ivory. There's something important I need to speak to Abatha about, and I hope you don't mind if we talk. Would it be convenient for me to have a word with her?"

"Maybe for you," Margaret said. "I've had nothing but calls for her today. From reporters, the police, even someone with the federal government. I'll tell you what I told them. She's not here right now. She's been out all afternoon."

"Shit," Arvo muttered.

Christine hushed him.

"Did you say something?" Margaret asked.

"No. Margaret could you take down my number and please call me when Abatha returns? It's very important that I speak to her."

"I'll add your name to the list."

Arvo motioned to Christine to put the phone on mute. "Find out who else is on the list."

Christine unmuted the phone. "Margaret. Thank you. Would you mind telling me something else?"

"Christine, I really don't have time. I've been on the phone all afternoon. I'm still expecting a call from a few more reporters. Can't it wait?"

"Margaret, I am really sorry for taking up your time. But could you tell me, please, who else is on the list? We may be able to help, somehow."

"You've really been no help at all, all of you down at the county. Bothering me at all hours. So much time driving Abatha in for these interviews and such."

Christine held off saying anything else. Arvo looked about ready to grab the Blackberry from her.

"Nothing but a nuisance, you people. I'll tell you once, then I really need to get back to my program, that is until the next person calls."

Margaret began reading names off the list, and Arvo frantically searched for something to write with and something to write on. Christine grabbed a pad and pen and began to take down names.

There were half a dozen reporters, several people from various departments at the county, all names either Arvo or Christine recognized. Then there was one name Margaret had difficulty pronouncing.

"Could you repeat that one, Margaret."

"Let me just spell it for you, the way the guy spelled it for me. He left a phone number, too. Masaryk. Jacob Masaryk."

"Thank you Margaret. We'll try not to bother you again."

She hung up and Arvo took the list and started to hurry out the door. "Wait a minute. Don't we need to find out who these people are?"

"No time for that now. We need to find Abatha first. Before anyone else does. They may have already listened to the tape of her interview, for all we know. They know where she likes to spend time."

They hurried out the door, reaching the elevator as it arrived, and though it went directly down without stopping, the floor numbers lit a slow-motion count down in slow motion that had Arvo pounding his fist on the wall and Christine inwardly cringing.

They reached the lobby and saw the place was crawling with reporters from all the media outlets, newspapers, radio, and televisions stations. Even the network affiliates were out in force. The sheriff was just taking his place in front of the microphones. A couple of reporters recognized Christine and Arvo from the night of the school presentation.

Microphones were stuck in front of Arvo's face.

"What do you know about the autopsy? Are there any new leads on the case Detective?"

"I'm sorry," he said, pushing away the microphones as he kept moving with Christine at his side. Then he stopped for a moment and turned to face the sheriff. "There's a reason I have nothing to tell you. I'm on leave. I'm not even assigned to the case anymore. You'll need to talk to the sheriff to get the status on the case."

The reporters turned away from him quickly and swarmed to the sheriff. Arvo and Christine were able to make their getaway without further attention from the media.

"We really need to move now," he said to Christine. "Damn these reporters."

"But what you told them, didn't it take the spotlight off you?"

"The media spotlight is really only a nuisance factor. But haven't you noticed, Christine? I'm sure you're being followed, just like me. I've been tailed the entire day by someone. I'm sure you have too. They're watching us walk to my car."

They got into the car, and Christine watched the direction of Arvo's eyes as he let her in the passenger side. Someone was watching and getting into another car on the opposite side of the parking lot.

"Buckle up, sweetheart. We're going to be booking down the back roads."

They drove off but not too soon to miss the sight of a beautiful young woman joyfully rejoining the family she'd been separated from for a few weeks. Christine watched as she clutched her parents in front of the cameras, now exonerated of two crimes: the one she didn't commit and the one she was accused of simply because of her status as a person of color and foreign birth. They would learn later that she'd brought the child to a crisis nursery within days of the baby's birth, after threats from her abusive partner. She'd been on her way to retrieve the child when she'd been taken into custody. Fearing that the baby would be unsafe in her abusive husband's hands, she'd said nothing when taken in by the police and was not offered a translator. The immigrant had done nothing but a selfless, courageous act of a true mother and suffered for someone else's heinous crime. Now, thankfully that was all behind her.

Ahead of Arvo and Christine lay a very twisted road to the truth, and Arvo was racing along it as fast as he could. Their best hope *if* they arrived at the other end, was that they'd find Abatha, unharmed. Finding the truth that existed beyond what she'd witnessed—like the sun that everyone knew lay beyond the heavy, unyielding atmosphere on a dim day like this one—would take longer. But they could all live with cloudy skies, and for a very long time. As long as Abatha was safe, it was bearable

19

CHRISTINE'S NEAT FREAKINESS usually gave her conniptions in a place like the Rolling Estates of Somerset Hills. They had the name right, she had often thought. The estates should be rolled right down the hills and into the river. The corrugated aluminum skirts were dented or missing on most of the trailers. The landscaping consisted mostly of junked cars, broken bicycles, and ramshackle swing sets. The poor taste, the general disrepair, and the tightly packed space, generally put her on the edge.

As Arvo was driving through the cramped, winding streets watching for Abatha's address, Christine was distracted enough to notice, for the first time, the small touches of tasteful decorating and landscaping. Tucked alongside some of the trailers were miniscule flower gardens bright with fall plantings of purple kale and orange mums and carefully bordered with hand-placed field stones. She saw an ivy-covered gate that led to a tiny backyard patio, crowded with ceramic planters and a quaint, antique iron table for two. In one bay window, she saw elegant crushed-silk drapes, an arrangement of late season lilies, and a lazy white Persian cat sleeping on a plump floral cushion. Abatha lived in this place, called it home, and despite the run down, decrepit look of parts of it, beauty had also found its small foothold there.

They arrived in front of Abatha's trailer, and Christine nearly cried to see it, looking so ordinary and homey. And so unprotected. Arvo knocked quietly at first, but no one answered. He knocked louder and still there was no answer. He looked at Christine and she held up her hands. She'd never come calling in a trailer court. She didn't know the protocol.

Margaret Cox didn't answer her door until the third knock, and by the third knock Arvo was banging on the door.

"Detective?"

"Yes, Margaret, I'm sorry to bother you."

"People have been banging at my door all day. Come inside." Margaret let him in, not seeing Christine at first, who hid herself behind Arvo and hurried to dry her face.

They entered Margaret's mobile home, walked a few steps through her kitchen, past a large aquarium which functioned as a divider between the kitchen and the living room, and then sat in her overstuffed reclining couch. Even though it was still daylight, she'd closed all her blinds. Her television was on, but the volume was low. Margaret was obviously trying to hide from the attention she was getting.

Christine reflected that she'd learned her lesson that night at the school. There was a consequence in getting a moment in the spotlight: you couldn't shut it off at will.

Arvo noticed the pad of paper with the names of callers on a small table.

"Can I offer you anything?" she said, apparently pleased to have their company. She was wearing a fussy sweater, the kind people gave away at white elephant holiday parties. It had thick multi-colored embroidery over a patchwork. The effect was like a poorly rendered paint-by-numbers. Her hair had been recently highlighted with thick bands of bleached blond and too ruby a red: the effect unfortunately looked like candy stripes radiating from her crown.

The phone rang and she ignored it.

"No, thank you, Mrs. Cox." Christine said, perched awkwardly on one end of the thick upholstery.

"Nothing for me, thanks."

Margaret looked away from her guests to the aquarium. The beautiful fish were gliding along in their safe, well-tended world.

She walked over to it and tapped on the side and one of the fish came to the glass to examine its reflection, attractively shimmering in the water. It fanned its tiny fins at the twin looking back at it. Mrs. Cox put her face right down near the glass.

"This is Abatha's aquarium. She takes exceptional care of the fish. She knows what kind of fish each one is, exactly when she got it, she keeps a little fish diary of things they do every day and how she takes care of them. She even keeps measurements of them."

"It's very nice. Somehow we're not surprised to see it. She seems very interested in animals," Arvo said. Arvo saw a computer sitting next to the aquarium. It was covered with pictures of birds and fish Abatha had cut from magazines or printed out from the web and taped carefully to the monitor frame.

"See, here's her notebook." She handed it to Arvo, and he paged through it. Abatha's notes and observations were meticulous. She had taped small pieces of tissue paper with each fish's outline on the notebook pages, which were cataloged by fish species. She'd even made some detailed drawings of each fish, and next to each drawing were details of where the fish was found in the wild, the habitat particular to the fish, and the date she'd added it to the aquarium.

Christine wondered at his patience with the older woman. For once, she wanted to be blunt and spit out what they came for without any delay.

"Mrs. Cox, Abatha wouldn't happen to be in, would she?" Arvo finally said.

"No, actually. She isn't back yet. She'd usually be back about now. It's getting to the dinner hour," Margaret said.

"How long has she been out?" Arvo said, looking at his watch.

"Oh. Most of the day. I let her stay home from school again. All of this bother from the news, it just gets the kids all riled up and she really doesn't like so much attention." Christine wondered if it was Margaret who decided she'd have enough attention.

"She went out in the morning, came back for lunch, and then left again."

The news was just coming on the television. Out of the corner of his eye, Arvo saw the sheriff reading the press release. Margaret looked at the television in time to see the immigrant girl being released into the arms of her joyful family.

"What happens now? Is Abatha going to have to be questioned again?"

"That's actually one of the reasons we're here. I'd like to talk to Abatha," Arvo put it that way. What he really meant to say was that he'd like to get her into protective custody, his alone or the county's. But he knew the county would not be as convinced as he was that she needed immediate protection. They'd act too late. And he wondered if that too late was already now.

"Mrs. Cox," Christine interrupted. "Do you happen to know where she might have gone?" Arvo shot her a look that told her he'd have preferred to handle things himself. She didn't care.

"Well, I'm not sure," she began as she sat on her couch and fluttered her hands on her lap. "I really don't know where the girl goes."

Christine felt her chest constrict. She wanted to throttle the woman, who had completely seemed to resign herself—from playing any role in nurturing the girl, or, at a minimum, keeping her safe from harm. And not just physical harm, but the emotional damage that raged around her, throughout her life, from the earliest age. The only reason Christine held back from giving Margaret a piece of her mind was that Abatha had been capably and stubbornly surviving, with her spirit and wits intact, despite all the odds. She could have done, and been, so much with more guidance and support from Margaret. And there was a real chance now that no one, not even Abatha, would have that opportunity, and go beyond just simply surviving.

The phone rang again.

"Don't answer it," Arvo said.

"But I need to, don't I? What do I tell these people who keep calling?"

"Nothing. Don't answer. Unless you see it's from me, the sheriff, or Ms. Ivory. We really need to leave now. We need to find Abatha. We'll be back in touch as soon as we know something. But please—no more talking to the press. No more talking to politicians. No more people you don't know. Please. Just no more talking."

Arvo and Christine drove out of the trailer court and down the dirt road leading to the river. They crossed under the graffiti-covered railroad bridge.

"I wanted to strangle that woman. How could you be so slow in getting anything out of her?"

"Didn't you see how upset she was, Christine? It was obvious she was worried. You didn't notice that?"

Christine didn't answer.

"Here's something else you probably didn't pick up. Did you notice anything strange about the drive to Margaret's house? The drive down here so far?"

"What?" Christine said, feeling her heart drop.

"Nothing. That's the problem. I didn't see anyone following us. I'd expected . . . I mean, while I didn't want to be followed here, at least it would have told me there was still a chance . . ."

Christine felt herself grow pale. "A chance of what?"

Arvo stopped himself from saying anything further.

Then she heard the little voice again. Arvo had gone silent and she knew he was hearing it, too.

Close to the river, right where I come to River Road and have to decide which way to turn, I looked for the eagles. If they are sitting on the dead tree branches right on the small island, then I turn left. If they aren't there, I turn right.

It was still easy to spot dead trees at this time of the year. The season was drifting down all around them: golden, scarlet and russet-colored trees were lit with the sepia of the autumn sun. Dead trees jutted up like the skeletal remains of some long gone species on a small island in the river.

That part of the road goes right next to the river, and there aren't many houses, so it's easier for me to get down to the shore. I like both directions, so that's why I always let the eagles decide for me. When they're there, I like to visit.

"There," Christine pointed. They saw the eagles sitting high in the trees, reading the fish from surface patterns on the opaque blue-black water below.

They turned left.

They drove along the river, and Christine watched as one eagle took off and swooped low along the river, as if they were following Arvo's car.

I could see the eagles perched on the treetops, and there is a place along the road where a narrow path takes you down to the river. There are a couple of big boulders there you can sit on, so I took that path when I came to it.

Arvo pulled over where he saw the narrow path, he knew it from an earlier visit there. He killed the engine and they got out. He came to the narrow path, Christine right behind him, then suddenly he stopped.

She looked down.

They saw them together. Footprints, large ones, from a man's shoes. The footprints made a path that went both to and from the shoreline.

"Stay on the edge, don't mess these up." They followed the trail down to the river. The big boulders Abatha had described were there at the edge of the water. Together they followed the footprints and when they reached the boulders, they looked carefully around it and saw smaller, faint footprints from a child's feet.

Bare feet.

The man's footprints led back up the hill, but the child's didn't. Christine hoped the return trail had been covered by the man's heavier footsteps. She tried to quell her fear that something worse had happened. Maybe Abatha had gotten away.

"Abatha!" Christine began to call. "Abatha!"

Arvo let her call, though he knew they wouldn't be answered. Christine began to search the shoreline, the edge of the woods, frantically calling.

"Why aren't you even trying, Arvo? She's got to be here, somewhere!" She grabbed him by his shirt and shook him. "You bastard. Come on, we don't have any time."

He put his hands on her shoulders, trying to tell her as calmly as possible. "We won't find her here."

"No! Of course, she's around. She's just hiding or looking for animals. You know her. Maybe she found a turtle she had to move somewhere." She began to turn away again. "A-ba-tha!" she said, raising the last syllable to push the call as far as she could.

Arvo caught her and held her more firmly. "Christine. You have to stop. She's not here. And you're damaging the crime scene."

"How can you be so sure that she's not here?"

Arvo gently guided her to the edge of one of the boulders and pointed to a few of the small footprints that appeared to have been lifted in flight, the heavy prints of the large shoes striding along. Then, the smaller footprints abruptly stopped, and were dragged along for a few feet, backwards, then they disappeared and the heavier shoeprints firmly marched back up the hillside.

"She's gone. We're too late."

It was Christine who fell to the ground sobbing this time, next to one of Abatha's delicate steps at the muddy edge of the water. She was wearing a simple cream-colored wool dress, with two plain wooden buttons along the back, and when she fell to the ground she looked like a battered piece of driftwood washed up by the river.

"Sweetheart," Arvo said to her. "We can't do anything for her here. You need to get up now."

Christine's dress was covered with mud, her face covered with tears, brown smudges from mud and mascara running down.

Arvo held out his hand.

"We can find her, right? We have to find her."

"You can count on it." Arvo tried to sound as sure as he could but he was not so sure. "I'll do everything I can. More." He kept his hand out.

At last she took it, for once allowing him to help her. As she struggled on the ascent up the narrow path, she began to lose her balance and felt his arm come around her, steadying her. She had let it happen, for the first time. She let someone else be in control. It was turning towards evening, a chill descended from the cooling air.

Christine shivered as Arvo helped her into the car and her teeth began to chatter until he put the key in the ignition. She willed herself to stop, but couldn't.

"I don't want her to be cold. They wouldn't let her be cold, would they?"

Arvo remembered the babies that had washed up on shore, and felt the horror of that cold grip of water on their unprotected, unwanted flesh. He shuddered. He knew he had to put his head around what had motivated Abatha's abductor, and all the possible places she might be found. This meant he had to visualize Abatha unprotected out there and in the hands of someone who could do her harm. He fought off a different sensation than the one Christine was struggling with. Nausea. He realized then that he needed to lie to her. "No," he said gently. "They wouldn't let her get cold."

He was sure that she pretended to believe him.

PART 3
RIVERBABY

20

THE CLOUDS, WHICH WERE ALREADY DENSE, thickened more, yet still were unyielding of any snow or rain as Arvo and Christine sped back to the Mendota County building. On their way, they were passed by numerous squads, lights flashing and sirens blaring, heading in the opposite direction back to the crime scene in response to the missing child alert Christine had immediately called in. Arvo had Christine make another call, to Juney, directing her to relate information about Masaryk and Abatha's computer. By the time they arrived at Arvo's office, Juney was ready with a status report of the ramped up activity.

"The Amber Alert went out. They've pulled everything they can find on this Jacob Masaryk. Lives in D.C. He's a Slovak national working with their government here in some capacity. Here's his picture."

"Thanks, Juney. As usual, you're a peach."

"By the way, the sheriff already called. Your leave is officially over, I take it."

Arvo grimly clenched his jaw, his eyes flashing on hers for a moment before he returned to business. "What do we have so far on Abatha's computer? Have they remoted in yet?"

"Close, Kieran's almost got it cracked. Go see for yourself."

Arvo headed out of his office and down a long corridor, Christine right at his heels. They entered the last room to the left, a cramped, dank basement filled with computers and cables. Except for the cracking sounds of police scanners, it might have been a college computer lab. A couple of young men and women were hunched over a variety of computers that were networked together through an intricate weaving of cables.

Arvo walked over to a tall, reed-thin, red-headed young man with thick glasses. He glanced up for a moment and Christine saw the neat cleft in his chin, marking his face with a sharp period.

Kieran called himself a code-geek. Arcane, difficult languages—whether they were software programs, spoken by tribes in remote jungles, or made-up by fantasy writers—were his specialty.

"What do you have for us Kieran?" Arvo asked.

"Just hacking into her social network profiles now. Her email and message logs will be downloaded next."

His fingers flew across the keys.

"What do you know about Slovakia, by the way?" Arvo enquired.

"Everything I just downloaded about it I could find. Check the screen to the right. I'm almost set here."

Arvo and Christine walked to the neighboring computer monitor and read the one page history. "In recent years, Slovakia has been pursuing a policy of encouraging foreign investment," Arvo read.

"Do we really need an economics lesson on eastern Europe? Now?" This was all taking too long.

Arvo took Christine aside, walking her out to the hallway.

"Christine, you need to get a grip." He put a hand on her arm.

She brushed it aside, but continued to listen.

"Look, I know this is a tough one. First, the death of a baby, for chrissakes. That was bad enough. Then, a second. "

Christine wiped the line of tears that began to spill over her eye lashes.

"And now, this. Abatha's gone."

She looked at him blinking.

"You *know*, Christine . . ." he said, putting hands on both of her shoulders. ". . . You *know* that you can't help a patient, a victim . . . if you let your emotions get the best of you. I know that you know that." He was emphatic, and gentle, in a way that he had never been with anyone, least of all her.

She looked down.

"Take a breath."

She did.

"Now, I need you to concentrate. I need you to remember everything Abatha's told you so far. I know it's not a lot. But anything can help."

Christine inhaled, raggedly. Then exhaled.

"Okay. Are you ready?"

They returned to the computer lab. From across the room a girl who looked hardly out of middle school piped up. She wore thick black braids and had freckles, a striking combination of black licorice and pepper. When she swung around, Christine saw she wore rainbow-colored knee highs that stretched over her knees, ending right at the hem of her plaid pleated skirt. Christine noticed she wasn't wearing shoes: each of her toes was covered by an individual toe sock. The middle-school look was a sharp contrast from exceptionally researched details she was quickly spitting out. Masaryk had been seen on Capitol Hill looking for an American military deal and Camryn already had a list of dates he'd been in various committee meetings.

"Apparently his company wants to get a contract going to build cluster bombs."

"Since when have we outsourced this type of thing, Camryn?"

"More often than you think."

"Is there any info on whether Masaryk has a connection with anyone around here?"

"See for yourself," Camryn offered, pushing her glasses up onto her freckled nose. She turned her laptop around. There, on the screen, was a photo of Senator Columbus-Powers standing next to Masaryk, shaking his hand.

"Well now. Isn't that interesting? And isn't it odd that Masaryk and Senator Columbus-Powers would be so interested in quality time with a girl who discovered a dead baby on the riverbank. What could possibly be going on there?"

"Something neither of them probably wants us to know," Christine offered.

Arvo gave her a smile.

"I'm in," Kieran announced. "Abatha calls herself Riverbaby on Facebook."

"And how do you know that?" Arvo said with a mock, unconvinced tone."

Kieran gave Arvo a look that said, "Come on, are you really questioning me?"

"I am just joking, but I forget how literal you are. Okay, just humor me, Kieran. Pretend it's your job to do that."

"I found her gmail identity and password and tied it to the account that way."

"Good boy. Now, for the class, tell us what we are looking at. Who's on her friend list?"

"There look to be, hmm, not many. She's a member of a whole bunch of animal groups. Oh, here's one friend. Recent. Mississippiboi."

"Bingo. Click on him."

"The birth year is missing. They seem to have chatted almost every day. From the sound of things, I'd say he's trying to pretend he's a kid."

"What makes you say that?"

"Abatha is obviously smart. This other person is trying to use a lot of acronyms, emoticons. Abatha never does. She's ignoring his remarks on her wall."

"Check her inbox."

Kieran clicked on Abatha's inbox. It was full of messages from Mississippiboi. "Open that one titled, "I saw you on TV.""

"*Y did they make U go on TV with that mean Snator. Its no fare.*"

"Did she write back?"

Kieran hit her sent messages tab. No. But here's her latest status update. From this morning. "*Grandma says no school today. Yay!*"

"See? Mississippiboi's response. He wrote on her wall."

"Lucky. I bet you be out of there all day."

"Did she say anything about that?" Christine asked.

"No. I get the impression she doesn't care for this person, whoever he is. He sent several messages to her inbox. He's chatty but she doesn't reply. Maybe she's on to him." Kieran clicked around to see if Abatha had posted recently on any of her group pages. Nothing had been updated in the last day.

"I would tend to agree with you. Mississippiboi seems innocuous, maybe harmless. Except we heard someone calling himself Mississippiboi has been hanging out in the strip joint. Do you have anything on Mississippiboi's IP Address."

"I'm surprised you know what that is, Arvo." Kieran said.

"Well now you're the one messing with me, Kieran." Arvo escorted Christine out, "Text me with any updates."

Evening had arrived early, brought on by the murky sky obliterating any remaining sunlight. It was even colder than it was before, a taste of what lie ahead in winter.

Arvo took one look at Christine. "You're a mess." She said nothing. "It's even worse than I thought—you weren't even offended by that remark."

Christine turned away. "I am offended," she complained tiredly. "I just don't even bother telling you anymore when you are insulting me. I figured I'd try ignoring you and see how that goes."

"Hoping that I would go away?" He smiled and scratched his stubbly cheek. "Tell you what, why don't I drop you at your place? I'll arrange to have someone pick you up in the morning."

"I'm still not sure I can trust you."

"Look, remember I was the one who practically carried you into your place after that night at the club. I think you can trust me. Let me, for once, help you out, Christine."

She got into his car and they drove in silence to her place. When they arrived at her building, she sat in his car, lost in thought and without any real idea what she could do anymore.

"What's next?" she said into her lap.

"The department is going all out to find Abatha. You know they are."

"I know." She sighed and leaned an elbow on his window. "What about the baby? The investigation."

"I need to make another trip out to the King of Spades, that's for sure. As soon as possible. Tonight."

"Tonight?"

"This kind of thing can't wait."

Christine straightened herself. "I want to come."

"I'm not surprised. You seemed quite interested in Mrs. Eide the last time we were there. Hoping for a repeat performance?"

"It's not that at all." She didn't bite, disappointing Arvo. "I'll drive myself crazy sitting here by myself. I don't want to be watching the Amber alerts crawling across the television set."

"Suit yourself."

"Just give me a few minutes to get myself cleaned up." She eyed him, her eyes glinting. "Because I'm such a mess."

"Fine."

Arvo parked the car.

"You might as well come up and wait inside."

"Well, this is unexpected," he said in a half-mocking tone.

"Do you want to come in? Or not? I'm not going to beg you."

He followed her inside, and as he hustled in to the elevator, he brushed against her awkwardly while each chose a corner of the elevator to station themselves.

"Pardon me," they both seemed to say at once.

She found her keys and let him into her apartment. "Make yourself comfortable," she said, showing him the way to her living room. "Can I offer you something, to drink?" she asked, knowing with Arvo it was like handing a live wire to a man with his feet in the water. She knew, equally, that she couldn't fix him.

"I'll get myself something. I assume the bar's over there?" he said, pointing to her kitchen.

"Yes," she said, heading at her bedroom.

Arvo wandered into her kitchen and found a glass, some ice, and some whiskey. He heard Christine start her shower and smelled the humidity filling the room. He walked over to her deck, opened the sliding glass door, and stepped out. He knew that below them the river valley opened itself up, inviting the stars to come out and shine over it, but the sky was still too overcast to let even the tiniest amount of light through. He could see, far below, a few streets winding through the valley, the head lights of a few cars driving along them. He thought of his ex-wife for the first time since early that morning, and realized how strange it was not to have her constantly in his mind, as she had been for months. He slowly sipped his drink, rather than slamming it down. He realized he didn't need the speedy numbness that he usually sought from a couple of fast-inhaled drinks.

A full day without obsessive thoughts of her crowding into his head was relief enough, even though the day had been full of more urgent activity. He wondered if there was a chance he was getting over her.

He came back in from the deck as Christine came out of the bathroom, wearing a robe, her hair damp. She stood still, watching him, with an unreadable expression on her face. Like the starless sky behind him, he had no clue what was going on in her head. She wasn't smiling, or angry, or even questioning him for once.

She just watched. And seemed to be waiting for him to make a move.

He walked to the kitchen and he noticed her following, without saying a word. He opened the cabinet where he had learned the glasses were kept, took another out, added a few ice cubes, and poured in a few shots of whiskey, then filled it to the rim with soda. He took another sip of his drink, and then held the other up to her, waiting for her to accept it from him. She did so, touching his hand lightly as she took it. She put the cool glass to her lips, moistening them as she slowly sipped the clear liquid. After she took that first drink, she leaned back against the counter, and laid her head back against the cabinet behind her, tilting her head to examine him.

He took another drink. He knew they should both be heading out as soon as they could, down to the club to find out more about Masaryk, but he was tired. He was so damn tired. He just wanted a moment of peace.

He could see Christine felt the same way: she was absolutely in no hurry. She lifted her glass again and took another slow, long drink, letting the whiskey sit on her tongue awhile before swallowing it. She watched him over the rim of her glass as she lifted it to her lips again, very gently laying the lip of the glass on her bottom lip. His eyes were locked on her as he watched the whiskey slip through her moist, parted lips. He set down his drink and moved closer to her, evaluating her, then leaned in, still not sure what to make of her opaque expression yet magnetized by her inviting mouth. His face came down on hers, his mouth drawn to hers, curious to taste her without any other pretense this time. There was no pursuer to fool. They had only each other to either deceive or come clean to.

The strange feeling of a different woman's mouth on his made a curious impression on Arvo. He knew Christine wasn't sure she wanted him and he wasn't sure he wanted her. Still, the kiss expanded, until it was an exploration of her face, then her neck. He inhaled the scent of a different woman's hair. His hands reached for Christine, opening her robe, then traveling around her waist to her naked back, pulling her closer to him. He felt her fingers unbuttoning then sliding under his shirt.

"What are we doing?" he mumbled at last into her ear, not as an objection but out of his recognition that he was unable to stop himself.

She had no answer, other than to gradually lead him into her bedroom, where their whiskey-moistened lips continued tasting, then exploring, then fully engaging the other dark, hitherto hidden areas of each other's bodies, until they were flowing in unison through an intense cascade, each knowing exactly how to reach the other side together.

They lay together on Christine's bed afterward, neither offering nor wanting excuses or explanations. Arvo let his hand run down the length of Christine's belly, to her thigh. In time she rose from the bed, and he began to gather his clothes. Christine allowed her dress to be zipped up by Arvo. And Arvo allowed his tie to be straightened by Christine. He pointed out where her mascara had smudged on the edge of her lid and she lent him a toothbrush. Arvo had the odd sensation of feeling as if they were a long married couple, comfortable in each other's flaws after years of living with the heartache those shortcomings had caused each other.

They were ready at last to head out. She made a final check in the mirror while he went around snapping off lights and rinsed their glasses in the sink. He held out her coat for her, she slipped it on, and he held the door, checking with her one last time to see that everything had been left just so. They were ready to face what lay ahead at the club.

21

ONDAY NIGHT AT A TYPICAL NIGHTCLUB was slow, but at the King of Spades, not so. Businessmen and politicians all needed a release from their weekends with the family. The just off the airplane local politicians needed to get away from the pressure of countless handshakes, baby kisses, and back-room deals. The salespeople and business coaches, in town for conferences, had freshly minted per diems to spend. With the financial system in the toilet, everyone economized by eating the cheap breakfast buffet at the hotel, hitting some fast food drive-through for lunch, and then splurging on extra drinks and a lap dance (or two) in the evening at the King of Spades.

They gave themselves the excuse that they deserved something, even if the company or the people were paying for it. They'd earned Mrs. Eide's dark-chocolate tease, maybe a trip back to the hotel with an escort. The King of Spades had a special account with a name on it that couldn't be linked to them. All that was required was money laundering through a few bogus accounts, maybe the occasional loan from the 401K that was kept in an Etrade account then paid off with something else. You just had to remember to get plenty of blank receipts you could write in bogus totals later—for cleaning, fictitious limo rides to the airport or taxi fares across town to dinner.

Arvo and Christine pulled up to a packed parking lot as a group of suit-jacketed business men came out for a smoke. Eide had strict rules about smoking in the club. Arvo had memorized the photo of Jacob Masaryk, but he didn't see him there with the group of anxious-looking men hunched over cigarettes. Obviously it was in between acts. No one came out during an act.

They went in and found a table where they could observe everything and not be seen. Eide had a number of private booths for personal entertainment, so they would have to be able to watch everyone to see if Masaryk was in. Arvo thought they had a fifty/fifty chance of spotting him. Christine had memorized the photograph, too. She was terrified of seeing anyone who looked like what she'd seen in the photo.

The Masaryk of the photo towered over the senator, which was not too difficult considering her small stature. Still, Arvo guessed he must be over six-foot-seven, but thin, so even at that height, a little over 200 pounds. His hair was shaved close to his head, and he had a dark outline of a widow's peak. Even though the man appeared around fifty, he looked like he'd never go bald, and when he did let his hair grow out, if ever, Arvo guessed his hair would be as thick as a bristle. His nose dropped heavily over his full mouth, in fact, all of his facial features were weighty, which seemed strange in a man so thin and tall. A shadow of a beard darkened his face.

"Do you want something, a drink?" Arvo asked Christine. "It's going to be a long night."

"Is that reason to drink? Or not?" Christine answered. She didn't regret coming with him, and was still recovering from what had happened between them in the last day.

"I'll get you your usual, although this time try and keep yourself under control," he winked.

"If you think you're going to control me, you can stop right now," Christine said, her irritation already flaring up again.

"You didn't need my help an hour ago. You had plenty under control."

Arvo was used to tender moments quickly slipping away: his years of abuse from Helen made it easy for him to conclude that Christine's mercurial mood made her just as cruel and he easily leapt to the conclusion that women were all alike. At least as far as he was concerned.

Still, she kept herself from leaving, and the waitress arrived and took their order.

"So my usual is a double Manhattan? You know me so well, now."

The stage lights colored just as their order arrived. Arvo got up to stroll through the club, knowing that everyone's attention would be directed to the stage. He carefully observed the audience members from a dark corner near the stage, the faces lit by the lights bouncing off the turning, bending, shaking flesh on stage.

All of the faces were tipped to the stage, and Arvo could even watch their eyes widen, their pupils move, showing each dilated interest in the carnal stage spectacle. The occasional twitch of a mouth. The slight movement of a nostril. Arvo looked for the enlarged nose, the full lips, a man with a pronounced widow's peak. He saw no one resembling the man.

Across the room he saw Vern Eide chatting with one of his scantily clad bartenders. He took a route across the club that kept him from interrupting the patrons' views of the show. He stopped to check on Christine, telling her he was going to the bar and would be back soon.

"Are you ready for a second?" he offered.

She shook her head. In her desire to thwart him, she was controlling the alcohol intake.

"Seen anyone we recognize yet?" Christine asked.

"Not yet. You?"

"Unfortunately a couple of my patients. That's why I won't be leaving this table anytime soon. I don't know if it's worse for me to see them or for them to see me."

"Might be good for them to see you. Bring a whole new flavor to the transference experience. I know it did for me."

"Would you quit it? That'll never happen between us again."

He headed to the bar.

"Vern," he said, acknowledging Eide with a handshake.

"Thorson, it's always good to see you. Jeanette, you remember Mr. Thorson, don't you."

Jeanette smiled, "Yes, of course. I hope he remembers me as well."

Actually, Arvo didn't, but nodded politely. Unfortunately there were probably too many women who remembered him too well.

"Eide, is the Mrs. around? I have a question or two to ask. I hope not to take up too much of her time."

Vern's expression darkened. Arvo watched his eyes dart around the club.

"Ahhm. I'm sorry to ask you to do this, but we've gotten a little attention. That we don't need. From the IRS. I'm a little uncomfortable giving you too much of her time. I don't need more attention."

"Buddy, you know me. You can trust me."

"How can I be so sure? Look, Arvo, I know we go back a ways. And pal I'd trust you with my life, but maybe not my business. Go back to that pretty friend you brought. I'll see what I can do."

Arvo ordered a couple of drinks from the underdressed bartender he couldn't quite remember.

She delivered them, and after Eide was out of earshot, she spoke. "Look, you don't have to fake it. I know you don't remember me. You're a good guy, Arvo, but a habit of yours (she said nodding at the drink) makes you forget important things. That girl you have over there has been watching us like a hawk since you left. Tell her she's got nothing on me. Don't screw her over like you did me."

"I'm sorry all I can offer you is an apology, Jeanette. I apologize a lot lately."

"No need to apologize. We had a good time one night. I'm sorry you don't remember that."

He returned to Christine.

"That bartender know you or something? She was flirting like crazy with you."

"Why, are you jealous?" He tossed back half his drink.

"Just get over yourself, Arvo. Just because we went to bed, once, means nothing. It was a weak moment, for both of us."

"A weak moment for both of us . . . what, does that make me some cheap one-night stand? You know what your problem is, Christine? You've got no one in your life, and as far as I know you never have. I have my problems, I know, and for me at least, I could be excused for a rebound, even with you. But god damn, woman, do you have to treat me like you've been married to me a decade and can hardly stand me?"

"What, you want to consider the events of a few hours ago to be some tender moment of passion between two lonely people? Fine. No one was taking advantage of anything, we'll just leave it at that."

The lights dimmed, and Christine was glad. She was furious and she knew she needed to settle down and keep an eye out for the thug that might have something to do with Abatha's disappearance. Her heart fell, thinking of the girl. It reminded her that what Arvo did have going for him was that he was a distraction for her, usually in their continued arguing, and now in bed.

Jeanette came to their table. "We have a special location ready for both of you, to enjoy the show in more privacy. Please, come with me."

They followed her, Christine trying to avoid being seen by the patients she recognized in the audience. Fortunately the darkness covered them. Jeanette took them to a door at the far side of the stage, and then led them down a hallway and up the stairs to a number of private suites. Each door had the name of a prominent hotel name on it—the Hilton, the Radisson, the Ritz, the Four Seasons, the Shangri La. She opened a door marked the Intercontinental and let Christine and Arvo in. The room had a window that looked out over the stage, a richly upholstered banquet, and a small bar.

"Compliments of the owner, please have whatever you wish and enjoy yourselves."

She closed the door behind them, and Arvo fixed a couple of drinks.

"Will anyone else be joining us?"

"What, are you afraid what might happen if we were left alone?" A sinuous medley of bump and grind filtered up from the stage and from above, the dancers seemed to move more slowly in a mysterious choreography of stimulation and raw desire.

He sat close to her, his hip next to hers, and reached over her to set the two drinks in front of them, his cheek brushing hers as he laid them on the table. Neither of them wanted to, but they turned to meet mouth-to-mouth, the desire taking hold without delay and as if the interruption of the past hour of bickering had only stoked the unbidden craving for each other.

Mrs. Eide entered the room from a side door, and without interrupting the passionate exchange inside. She was used to making a quiet entrance and the loud music drowned out many of the sounds that might come from these rooms. Mr. Eide wanted his customers comfortable and their passion kept anonymous.

Arvo saw her first, and pulled away gently from Christine. Christine followed his mouth and nearly fell into him, finally noticing they weren't alone.

"I'm terribly sorry to interrupt you, but I heard you wanted to talk to me? Hello, Ms. Ivory. I'm glad to see you enjoying our establishment again."

Christine straightened herself. She didn't quite know whether to acknowledge Mrs. Eide's polite remarks, or to keep her distance, as false as that was. She decided that she would put some space between herself and Arvo. Mrs. Eide bestowed a mysterious and non-judgmental smile on her.

"Thank you for the hospitality of this suite. It's very . . . nice." Christine heard herself say.

"You're very welcome." She moved into the room, smoothly with graceful movements that were not exactly a dance, but not exactly walking either. Christine hadn't quite decided whether Mrs. Eide was a normal human like herself and Arvo. She did understand how she could have saved Mr. Eide's life.

"What is it you wanted to know?"

Arvo removed the copy of the newspaper from his jacket pocket. "Would you mind looking at this picture and let me know if you've seen either of these people?"

Mrs. Eide took the paper in her hands and straightened the folds out of it. She drew her long fingers across the page and put a manicured nail under the gentleman's face.

"Yes, we do see this gentleman occasionally in the club. Actually he came in within the last week."

"You wouldn't happen to know his name, would you?"

"You certainly don't need to ask me, his name is on the page as anyone can see." Mrs. Eide's expression had not changed, but Christine detected a subtle hesitation.

"I can certainly understand your wish to keep the patrons' names anonymous," Christine asked as gently as possible, "and please understand that we wouldn't be asking you if it wasn't a matter of the gravest importance. If you don't want to let Mr. Thorson know, for professional reasons, perhaps you can tell me, for personal reasons."

Mrs. Eide considered the request, and hesitated only a moment longer. "You already know the name I know him by. I believe you mentioned it the last time you enjoyed our facilities."

"Mississippiboi?"

Her beautifully arched brow answered. She turned to leave. "I assume you need nothing more from me, so I will leave the two of you to continue your conversation."

She left as quietly as she entered, but both Arvo and Christine knew that the conversation between them needed to end that evening. The two dots had been connected with at least a faint line. They looked down at the newspaper clipping left behind. Now a third dot had been connected, with a much bolder line, though it was still unclear why, and when they would learn how, or if, it might lead them to Abatha.

22

THE NEWS ABOUT ABATHA'S disappearance instantly hit the twenty-four/seven news cycle, even at the national level, and Christine found it impossible to tune it out. When she arrived at her mother's apartment the next day after work, naturally it was on every channel on her television set, either scrolling across the bottom of the screen or in bold, screeching CNN headlines.

Still no word on the missing girl, Abatha Cox, last seen yesterday. Her grandmother Margaret Cox, seen with Abatha in this footage from Senator Columbus-Powers campaign event at Somerset Hills elementary school, did not accept our request for an interview. On the campaign trail with the senator, whose closely contested race is coming to the finish line, our reporter Chad Winston asked the senator about the missing girl she spent time with just days ago . . .

CNN cut to scene of Senator Columbus-Powers with the microphone in her face . . . *a terrible tragedy, what that poor little girl has been through already. Our prayers go out to her family and we hope she is returned soon and safely.*

"What is wrong with those people down there?" Dorla Ivory clucked. "First they're tossing babies into the river, now a poor little girl is missing. I don't know why you still have anything to do with that town! I left the place as soon as I could . . . and even then I stayed too long." Dorla Ivory went on non-stop and Christine didn't have to pretend to interact.

While her mother carried on, Christine boiled some pasta and threw together a quick sauce with sautéed onions, garlic and herbs and a can of chopped tomatoes. She sliced the loaf of Italian bread she brought and called her mother to the counter when everything was ready.

Her mother tore into everything, even though she had protested once again she wasn't hungry. "What's with you today, Christine? You haven't said a word since you came in."

Christine was surprised she noticed. "Everything's fine, Mom."

"What on earth are you wearing?" Dorla leaned over the counter and looked Christine up and down. "Oh, my word. You in jeans? I haven't seen you in jeans in years. And your roots are showing. I'm calling Lorraine right now, Christine," she said picking up the phone. "You need some proper color in your hair, not that whatever it is you have going there with the black and blond streaks. A proper beautician like Lorraine will fix you up in no time."

"Mom. Put down the phone. I'm over forty now. You don't need to make my appointments."

"Well, you should think about it. Lorraine would fix you right up, and give you a perm. You need something. Why so down in the dumps? Have you got yourself a boyfriend, yet? Weren't you going out on a date last week?"

Christine tried to remember what she might have told her about going out the last week. Had she mentioned something? Maybe she was broadcasting more than she thought.

"Mom. It's nothing. Really."

"Well, it doesn't seem like nothing. But of course you never talk to me. We barely see each other."

Christine knew that wasn't even close to the truth.

Behind her the television set continued blaring about the unsolved crime and the missing girl. She suddenly heard Arvo's name and turned to the television, dropping her fork.

What can you tell us about the progress of the investigation, Detective?

Dorla Ivory turned up the sound. "That's Arvo? Didn't he go to school with you?"

"Mother, be quiet. Please."

Arvo spoke. "The investigation is ongoing and we really can't comment. That would jeopardize the case."

Behind him, Christine could see the sheriff.

"Does the girl's disappearance have anything to do with the ongoing investigation?" one reporter said, jamming the microphone in front of Arvo and barring his way.

Arvo pushed the microphones away and kept moving, not even bothering to say, "No comment."

Another reporter jostled in front of Arvo. "How did the department blow it so badly taking in the wrong person, and on such obviously non-existent evidence?"

"I don't know anything about that. I wasn't involved."

"But aren't you the lead investigator on the case, Detective."

"At the time, I apparently wasn't. I have nothing more to say to you," Arvo said, moving out of camera range. The reporters rushed to the sheriff, shoving microphones in his face.

"Can you tell us more about the lack of progress in the investigation?"

Christine left her mother sitting in front of the television set, grabbed her things, and headed out the door, but not soon enough to miss her mother saying, "Christine, you just got here. You haven't even finished the dishes."

Christine slammed the door behind her.

Less than an hour later, Christine stormed into Arvo's office without even bothering to knock.

"He's not in," Juney said from a few feet behind her. "Do you always make such a dramatic entrance?"

"Where is he?"

"Ms. Ivory, I believe your office is somewhere in the stratosphere, above our sad little suite."

"Where is he?"

"Really. Is this a personal call or a professional one?"

Christine didn't answer. She turned and left.

"Shall I mention you dropped by?"

Arvo appeared a few minutes later.

"You just missed the good social worker."

Arvo almost snapped at her. "I've had as much sarcasm as I can stand. Don't start with me."

"What is going on with the two of you, anyway?"

"Where's that article with the picture of the senator and the Slovakian."

"I gave it to you, don't you remember?"

"Dammit I can't find it anywhere," he said, shuffling through the papers on his desk and slamming file drawers. The printer connected to his computer suddenly fired up. It spat out a sharp copy of the photograph.

Kieran stood in his doorway. "I heard you were missing something."

"Thank you," he grumbled, waiting for the printer to finish.

"High resolution, just for you. By the way, don't thank me, thank Juney."

Juney stood behind Kieran with a blank expression on her face.

"Sorry. Thanks Juney. I'm pissed off and apologize for my lack of respect."

"Lack of respect? Fine, I accept."

Arvo grabbed the picture and ran out.

"See you later?" Juney said as an afterthought.

Kieran said, "I see he's in a chipper mood today."

"No, Arvo, we can't drag a senator in for questioning. On that? A picture?"

Arvo leaned over the sheriff's desk, practically in his face, his finger gunning on the inkjet print that had barely dried.

"I told you. This is the guy who Margaret Cox said called her the day Abatha disappeared. What the hell is a guy like this doing calling on a kid?"

"The Slovakian we can bring in, obviously. If we can find him. Not the senator."

Arvo insisted. "Something is bothering me about the level of interest the senator has had in this kid all along. At one point, before we have someone in custody—the wrong someone—she's all sincere to the point of making goo-goo eyes at the girl, as if she's ready to adopt her for some cause."

The sheriff listens.

"Then, ta-da, the night of the bullshit media event over the school, she's right on spot for the six pm news cycle to announce someone has just been arrested, wrongly, but the perfect example for her bullshit agenda."

"Arvo, you're connecting a lot of things that aren't connected."

"They are, though you don't believe it." He aims his finger at the picture again. "I know for a fact that this man has been seen here in town, and recently. I have reason to believe that he's been contacting Abatha, and only in the past week or so. And not just the one phone call to her grandmother."

"Care to elaborate on those reasons you have to believe there's more of a connection?"

"No, I can't. Not now."

"Arvo you always get us in this position. Your unnamed sources. We end up with nothing we can actually tie together."

"I only need more time. And the senator."

"You still haven't convinced me why the senator has anything to do with this. Other than this picture from months ago."

"I know that. But here's the thing. Suddenly we have no one in custody. We're starting over. Abatha disappears. And the senator, who was so interested in the welfare of this poor child, says something straight out of the PR script—a 'terrible' tragedy. Bullshit. She's trying to get herself out of this mess. It really screwed up her political agenda to have that girl released. Now she's trying to stay as far from this town as she can. First she's got a baby being murdered in her home town, now the disappearance of a girl in her home town, and no one to blame that she can spin into her agenda."

"Arvo you can't have someone brought in for questioning just because you don't agree with their politics. Remember, this is a democracy. We have the various freedoms. You and I are here to protect and defend."

Arvo pulled away from the sheriff's desk.

"We'll get the Slovakian brought in. That's the most we can do."

Arvo got up and began to turn away.

"One more thing, Arvo. Please."

Arvo stopped but didn't turn around.

"I brought you out of your leave, early. I'm not convinced you are entirely ready to be back at work. I've seen nothing from any doctor releasing you back to work."

"My personal life is none of your business. Do you have any professional complaints you want on my record?"

The sheriff had nothing to say. Arvo faced him and waited. The sheriff drummed his fingers on his desk. "You know you're the number one in this office. But you are right on the line, always, with how you approach investigations. And now this—" he said picking up the photograph and pitching it back across his desk "—flimsy evidence that you bring to me, expecting me to haul a United States senator in for questioning. Arvo, I get tired of riding herd on you. Do you know what might happen if this went wrong? I bring in a senator and it turns out there's nothing. Then my ass is on the line. Don't you get it?

Arvo stood with his hands on his hips.

"No. You never get it. At some point I'll give you enough rope and you'll hang both of us."

"As long as we're swinging together, Bill. We'll invite all our friends. They'll be partying like crazy."

Ruud didn't smile. "We'll get someone on that Slovakian. We'll call you when he comes in. We'll find him."

23

I HEARD YOU WERE LOOKING FOR ME," Arvo said, breezing into Christine's office the next morning like he owned the place. "Miss me?"

Christine had gone home stewing about Abatha . . . and Arvo. But she told herself it was mostly Abatha who'd upset her thoughts. She'd worked hard that night trying to restore order to her soul. She took it out on her closet, rummaging through everything, taking out the summer things, tossing some things in bags meant for charity, and getting her winter wardrobe out.

She realized she was tired of obsessing, and naturally she worked through it by obsessing more. She'd grown bored of her usual wardrobe palette. Yes, her mother was right, her roots were showing. She didn't care. She took a scissors to her hair and chopped it off in a blunt, uneven line. Then she went at it with a razor blade to create an uneven jagged end at the nape of her neck. She did the same at her brow.

There wasn't much from her wardrobe she was remotely interested in wearing. Even black, which might have some redeeming value just because it was a non-color, wasn't working for her. Finally, when she came up with something to wear the next day, it was past midnight and her bedroom was strewn with clothing. She fell into bed exhausted, but slept fitfully.

She slipped on the delicately crocheted caramel-colored dress the next day. The bronze highlights she haphazardly streaked in her hair picked up the theme. She grabbed metallic colored shoes from her closet, a chain metal purse, and she was ready. To the uninformed, the combination wouldn't have immediately suggested itself. On Christine, the metallic cast to everything molded onto her like armor. She was ready for a crusade.

"Why hasn't that child been found yet? All over the news they're saying the whole case has been screwed up from the start. That you and the sheriff don't have your act together. How badly bungled is this thing anyway?"

Arvo gave her a once over. "I'll take that for a 'yes' as in 'yes, you missed me.'"

Christine realized that she couldn't read his tone anymore. It sounded like he almost wished she had missed him, though cutting through his thick layer of sarcasm was difficult.

"I'm waiting for an honest answer, Arvo," Christine said. He stood in the middle of her office, challenging her just by the fact that he was here and he'd seen her in vulnerable moments. She felt he was pushing her into making a bold move. What, did he think she was just going to get up and fall into his arms? Or start crying?

"So am I, Christine. But I see I'm not going to get it, so I'll attempt to answer your naïve question. You should know better. Look, I'm as frustrated as anyone. But the sad fact is that these things take time."

"Arvo, let me make the same lame statement that the press is taking. The girl doesn't have time. Why isn't any progress being made?"

"Progress is being made, it may not look like it. We have a lead on the Slovakian. With any luck, he'll be in for questioning today."

"And, in typical style, your department will screw up and he'll have been long gone."

"Why do you think all I'm capable of is failure?" Arvo asked, throwing up his hands, but not budging an inch.

"What evidence is there to suggest otherwise?" Christine answered.

"What's your problem with me? You never give an inch, even when there are moments of—whatever you want to call what happened between us the other night. And actually now you've gotten harsher with me."

"Look. My criticism is justified."

"No, it's not Christine. When I've screwed up, I'm the first to admit it. You know I had nothing to do with that earlier snafu. You know I'm the most decorated investigator in the county, despite some handicaps which I won't discuss here."

He squared on her face and motioned a line connecting the two of them. "This—problem we have . . ." he said, drawing a line between them with his index finger ". . . this goes back a long way, almost ever since we've known each other."

Christine remembered. Indeed it had gone back a long way.

"Admit it. You've always hated me. I don't know why. Well now I'll ask you. I need you to work closely with me on this case. Whatever is stuck between us is only going to get us hung up when we really need to be able to team up. And don't roll your eyes when I say that."

Christine finally stood up from her desk and went to her window, her back to him. Should she admit where her feelings were coming from? Outside her window, the trees were almost completely emptied of leaves with bare branches exposed everywhere. She wasn't sure whether she should tell him anything. She wasn't sure why her irritation with him had grown. All she could do was reveal the raw feelings.

"I can't remember when it started, but I've always hated you. Since way back." She turned and faced him. "Maybe 'hated' isn't the right word. Let's say strong negative feelings. I don't feel any need to apologize for it."

"So do I at least get an explanation? In fact, I demand one. What have I done to deserve your anger? Did I stand you up on a date? Not call back? We know neither of those is possible."

Christine had her reasons. She knew it sounded more like pity for herself. She wasn't sure she should trust him with the story, but decided at last to try and tell him anyway.

"My father left the family when I was around Abatha's age. As far as I could tell, it amounted to nothing more than boredom. He was tired of being married, tired of having a family. It was all such a come down from the glory of his high school days. He was the king of everything, led everyone, you know, dated the homecoming queen. Not my mother, incidentally. They married after she found herself pregnant with me. He cheated on everyone, even the homecoming queen. I'm proof of that."

"So, boom, that means you hate Arvo? Poor woe is me fatherless Christine? You resented someone who was so much like your own father and then throw all of that onto me? For years?"

"Let me finish telling my story. Since you insist. Look, I know as well as anyone that this story sounds like a lot of ungrounded resentment and bitterness. Helen treated me like crap back then, too, her and all of her little cheerleading girlfriends. I decided right then and there that she, and you, put that line of barbed wire up where I was on one side—uncool and never worth the time of people on your side. I decided then and there my mission was to blow past all of you."

"... this explanation still isn't personal enough and you know it. Even I'll give you chops for being above petty school girl resentment. What, specifically, did I do?"

"A lot of small things, Arvo. I think you only need examine your own memory, if it still exists, and you'll find the version of you I saw in those days. To stay the king, you need to keep a strong arm on the peasants. I was one of those peasants, in your view.

"All I can remember, Christine, is being stoned or drunk or both. A few rare occasions, I wasn't and they coincided with important events, like the homecoming game and the SAT testing days. Wait, let me correct that. I remember you, watching me with your condescending, dismissive look, kind of like the one you have now. Let me give you an alternate perspective. Maybe you did like me, but for the wrong reasons. If I did remind you of your blessed deserting father, maybe you thought that I should just come to my senses, notice you, remember I could be a better self. Maybe you thought I could be fixed. I really felt like there was nothing wrong with me. In fact, even in my stoned haze, I was sure I was at the top of the world. In love with my beautiful girlfriend, star quarterback, SATs that could get me anywhere. Yet, I went nowhere. I didn't need you then, Christine."

He came to stand next to her and leaned in close to her neck, breathing on her as he said it. "I won't need you tomorrow."

His lips touched her neck. "I don't even need you now."

"You just can't stand not being able to control me. Or your father. Even with everything you know about people and how they think."

Christine didn't move, held in place by the magnetic pull of Arvo so close to her. Maybe he was right. And the jolt he gave to her system, painful and powerful. She needed it.

At last she broke away. They both stood and stared at each other like a pair of prize fighters pulled apart by a referee. Both acknowledge the other's power and their inability to finish each other off.

Arvo felt his phone buzzing in his pocket. A text from Juney. It shocked the raw look out of his face. "They've found Masaryk and brought him in."

"I'm coming with you."

Arvo said nothing to her, but held the door open behind him. She hit the elevator button and they both got in.

Masaryk was processed and being held for his interrogation by the time they arrived. Arvo had read his processing papers in the hall, with Christine glancing over his shoulder.

Jakob Masaryk, aged forty-seven, Slovak Republic national, controlling interest in Antonik Korporácia, located in Bratislava, the Slovak capital. Divorced, children unknown, parents deceased. His passport showed visas for many European capitals and various business trips to the United States. He gave a Washington, D.C., address as his current residence.

"Do you think this guy has anything to do with Abatha's disappearance?" Christine asked.

"I'm going into interrogation with that assumption in mind. We'll see."

He opened the door of an adjacent room, and showed Christine in. Together they looked through the one-way mirror and saw Masaryk, hunched over the table, chewing his knuckles. He hadn't changed from the photo as far as either could tell. In fact it appeared he was wearing the same frayed, wrinkled suit.

"Did you get a look at the guys chasing us at all?" Arvo asked Christine.

"I was going to ask you that question."

"I want your thoughts."

"I noticed the driver seemed tall. His head touched the ceiling of the car. Think that could be the guy?"

"It was too dark to get a really good look at him. At least during the chase. But they did come inside looking for us at the club, if you remember."

"You were blocking my view that night, as I remember it." Christine said.

Arvo remembered, and flashed on another memory of Christine blocking his view and pretty much everything else, a few days earlier. He forced his thoughts back on the ugly guy on the other side of the glass from Christine.

"From the glimpse of them I got, I'm pretty sure he is our pursuer. The height is a dead giveaway. But if he was after us, before the immigrant girl was released and before Abatha disappeared, why? What did we have, that he needed?"

"Well we never did give him a chance to get whatever he was looking for. I'm sure as hell going to try to squeeze something out of him now."

Arvo left Christine and entered the interrogation room. When Masaryk saw him, Arvo noticed no sense of surprise or recognition on his face. The man knew how to keep his hand to himself.

"You don't have anything on me. I do have some rights, you know."

"Mr. Masaryk, thank you for your time. I'm glad that you were informed of your rights."

"If you call what the police who dragged me in here told me, then you are misinformed. I am a citizen of the Slovak Republic. We do not, even in our state, take lightly what your police have done by bringing me in such a manner into your office." Masaryk had, in fact, said something far more direct and coarse in his language to the police officers. The cops were easily able to translate what they heard, with absolutely no knowledge of Slovak. They'd been pretty much called everything in every language over the years, and knew when they were being insulted.

Masaryk said he had friends in high places, he didn't name them, but he would if he needed to.

"You are not being charged with anything at this time. You are a person of interest by virtue of your contact with Margaret Cox the day that her granddaughter Abatha Cox disappeared. We need to follow up on any lead related to her disappearance."

"Yes, all of that was explained to me," Masaryk stated bluntly, waving his hand dismissively. "My cooperation is respectfully requested . . . ad nauseum. I am a businessman. I have nothing to do with this little girl."

"Then why does Mrs. Cox have you listed as a person calling her residence the day her granddaughter disappeared. Yes, we have her telephone records showing a phone call was placed to her from a cell phone number. We can certainly go to the trouble to get your cell phone records to corroborate that the phone number on her telephone records matches the cell phone number of record for you, though probably that will be more difficult given the efforts some take to mask their identity."

"I don't know why Mrs. Cox would have noted my name, in particular, on that day. A businessman from my part of the world has many relationships. Sometimes one makes enemies. This is unfortunate. Perhaps one of my enemies wants to link me to this poor unfortunate girl's disappearance. And make trouble for me. It is a difficult business climate and unscrupulous people will take advantage of that, in any way that they can."

Masaryk was tap dancing, and doing it very well, especially for a man of his size and apparent lack of agility. Arvo was ready for the next step. He took out the newspaper article with the photograph of Masaryk standing next to the senator.

He laid the photograph in front of Masaryk and smoothed out the wrinkles. He watched Masaryk's expression to see if he could detect any change.

"I assume you will want me to comment on this photo," he said, sighing as if completely bored. He leaned over the table and looked at it, sliding his glasses up over his forehead to make plain the extent of his far-sightedness and the effort they were putting him through.

"Oh, yes. The senator. She and I spoke of a business opportunity and whether the United States would like closer connections with Slovakia as part of that business opportunity."

"And this is why you've recently been in the senator's state, just to pursue a business opportunity?"

"Yes, of course." He pushed the photo back to Arvo angrily.

"And that business opportunity involves contacting a young girl?"

"You talk in circles, Detective."

"Do your business opportunities often require contact with young girls?"

"Exactly what are you insinuating, Detective? Are you trying to insult me?" Masaryk sounded genuinely irritated. Arvo knew he was narrowing in on some truth, though Masaryk could just as easily have determined showing his real irritation would still reveal nothing.

"I know that some people think my part of the world is vulgar and that sometimes life is treated cheaply. Mr. Thorson, let me tell you, honestly, that when one is in business in my part of the world, yes, it requires more risks that mere money. One must have the temperament to do all of the work that is required, and sometimes that work can make one do ugly things one wishes one did not have to do."

He paused and slid his glasses up, looking Arvo straight in the eye. "I have not laid a hand on that child."

There was a knock at the door, and a police officer handed Arvo a note. It was from Christine. "The bracelet."

He folded the note and put it in his pocket, keeping a watchful eye for Masaryk's reaction. The man seemed to barely blink.

"Mr. Masaryk, no one asked you for a lecture on the business dynamics in eastern Europe."

"I beg to differ," he interrupted.

Arvo pushed the photograph back in front of Mr. Masaryk and observed him again. The man sat back in his chair, an angry expression growing on his face. "Look again at the picture. Isn't there more you can tell me about the relationship between you and the senator? What has come out of your talks so far?"

Masaryk angrily pushed the picture away again. "Nothing. The senator has, in fact, broken off negotiations entirely. She has stopped returning my calls."

Arvo arched a brow. He'd found his target in the genuinely bitter attitude of Masaryk's statement.

"Interesting. I've heard she's on a certain committee, with a lot of sway. It would seem she's exactly positioned to do the right thing for you."

"She certainly is," he almost spit. "At one time she was ready to help me, practically begging me to open my wallet so she could stuff cash into it."

"And now?"

Masaryk looked as if he was about to answer, his face growing red, then suddenly remembered where he was. The air went out of him.

"This is how business works," he said with resignation. "I think Americans put it this way: one step forward, two steps back. Sometimes it is straight forward. These things take time." He was deflated, and sweating. "What more do you need to ask me? I'm a business man, this is taking up much of my time."

"I am very appreciative of your time. I will have a word with the officers that brought you in here, they may have been more harsh with you than you deserved."

"Thank you. You are an understanding gentleman. Tough, but understanding."

"There is one more thing. If you wouldn't mind. This won't take much of your time." Arvo subtly changed his tone to one less adversarial, more conspiratorial. The difference was nuanced. Too much a shift would have been detected, and considered artificial, not to be trusted.

Masaryk listened as if he was beginning to trust.

"Something else is missing. Along with the girl. It may be connected. Or it may not be connected. I want to tell you about it, because I know you are in contact with many people. If you happen to hear where it might be, it would help tremendously in many ways, if you let me know."

Masaryk leaned forward, slightly.

"A small, silver, beaded bracelet."

The eyes shifted away, just momentarily. Then shifted back.

"Probably not more than an inch or two in circumference."

"I don't deal in jewelry, Detective. There's little chance I'd come across such a delicate piece." The businessman couldn't resist. "Is it valuable?"

"It may be. Depending upon who finds it. And when."

"I will be of little help to you, Detective, of that I am quite certain." The dismissal seemed veneer thin, and they both knew it. "If by chance I come across it, and that is a very small chance. I'll consider bringing it to your attention."

"That's all I ask" Arvo said simply, though his tone suggested he expected much more. "In my line of business, it's all a matter of timing. Someone turns up something at the right time, and in the right way, and it can be a win-win situation."

Masaryk's eyebrows bristled. "Yes. I see. That is what we work towards in business. A win-win situation. All are benefited."

"Exactly."

Juney was waiting for Arvo when he came back to the office. Christine was with him.

"Get your man?" she asked.

"Are you asking her or me?" Arvo said.

Juney made a face. Arvo didn't look to see if Christine had made a similar face.

"You know how these things go . . ." Arvo said.

"Well, I don't. He practically gave the guy a free pass? How come you didn't push harder on the phone call to Margaret? The fact that the guy almost ran us off the road? Meanwhile, Abatha is still out there, somewhere. This does nothing to help her."

"Settle down, Christine. Arvo's right," Juney said. "If I know him, he's set something in motion." To Arvo she said, "Kieran turned something up."

"That's my boy. What?"

Juney led the way back to Arvo's office, where a new print out lay on his desk. "This is a picture of the senator and her daughters."

"So a photo of the senator and her daughters. What he did a Google image search? This does nothing for me." He tossed the paper back onto his desk, noting that Christine's eyes had followed it.

"I don't know everything, Arvo. The other info Kieran located said something about the oldest girl, Laura, heading off to do some studying abroad in the spring. She turned up again recently."

"Kids that age, especially kids with parents like that have always gone off to study elsewhere. Nothing new there. Is Kieran losing his touch or something?"

"He said you'd want to see this photo. In particular. He didn't explain why. What, am I the go between for the two of you now?" Juney looked as if she was ready to give up.

"Let me see that," Christine said, making a grab for the picture. She turned the sheet around, and Arvo watched her zero in on one of the senator's daughters, the eldest, a girl who looked to be in her late teens. The picture had been taken the past winter, at some gala celebration in Washington. The senator was smiling at her daughters, all dressed in ball gowns.

Christine looked up, her face pale.

"What is it?"

She said, "Look at the oldest one."

She held the paper up to Arvo's face, her hand shaking. Arvo had to take it from her in order to see clearly what she was trying to point out. Juney came to his side.

"Around her arm . . . wrist, I mean."

The girl was small, like her mother, and around her wrist was a small, unusual silver bracelet. A shiny beaded bracelet.

"That can't be . . . possible. I mean, a lot of girls are into jewelry," Juney said. "There's got to be tons of it out there."

"It seems like the kind of thing made for a child, not a girl that age. Especially with a ball gown. I don't know. Maybe it's nothing." Christine evaluated the photo closely, her fashion sense remembering how sharply dressed the senator was. She would have wanted what her daughters wore to make a statement. She wasn't the type of woman to leave anything out of place, damaging the public image.

"I don't think it's nothing. Unfortunately, the only person who has seen the missing bracelet is missing herself," Juney said.

"Then we better move on our next steps in finding her. Juney, have Kieran blow this up. We want to get a closer look." Juney gave him an "excuse me," look.

"Actually. Give me that. Never mind, I'll go tell him myself."

Arvo headed off leaving Juney and Christine in his dust. Juney gave an interested look in Christine's direction, smirking.

"Do you have something to say to me?"

"Yes, as a matter of fact. Maybe you know. What's gotten into him, lately?" Juney said, tossing out some bait lightly, not expecting it would get her anywhere.

"Why on earth would you think I'd know?"

"Well, for instance, the two of you seem to be keeping quite a bit of company lately."

"For business-related reasons, let me be perfectly clear on that." Christine was surprised by quickly rising to her own defense. If she had nothing to cover up, then she should have had nothing to say. She realized she'd spoken up too quickly.

"Oh. I see. Business reasons. Of course. The two of you are huddled over business. I suppose you meet for cappuccinos and discuss your casework."

"Is everyone in this office completely infuriating?" She stomped off.

Juney laughed as she left. "Business reasons. Right."

To prove the point, Christine headed to the computer lab. Arvo was standing next to Kieran, pointing at the photo when she arrived in the doorway. Everyone looked up, even the smarty-pants geek girl. They could see Christine obviously had nothing to bring to them.

"I need you to do one more thing for me, Kieran."

"What's that?"

"Do you still have access to Abatha's Facebook account?"

"Like I wouldn't? Do you know me after three years yet?" Kieran hacked into her account.

"Is there a way you can make it look like it's been updated? Like she's still accessing it."

"You mean update her status and comment on her friends' pages?"

"If that's what you call it, I suppose. Yes that's what I mean. What makes the most sense? What would lead someone to believe that she's alive and kicking, like nothing happened."

Kieran looked at Arvo a bit peeved, but attempted some patience. He talked to him slowly, as if he was talking to an elderly, completely unhip person. "That would be to update her status. Is that what you want me to do?"

"Show me where that is."

Kieran pointed out the various areas of Abatha's Facebook page, including various areas of her profile, her interests, her beliefs. Abatha had uploaded pictures of animals on her photo page. Her page hadn't been updated since she disappeared.

"Come up with something that would sound like other statements she's made on this page."

Kieran thought for a moment, then went to the field that listed Abatha's last Riverbaby status. A box read "What are you doing now?" Christine walked up and looked over his shoulder.

She asked him if she could type in a status for Abatha.

"Be my guest," he said, standing up from the chair and holding it out for her. She sat put her fingers on the keyboard. She knew in a moment what Abatha might be doing and typed it in without delay.

Riverbaby is looking for the eagles.

24

CHRISTINE STARTED THE NEXT DAY in the lowest spirits she'd felt in weeks. Abatha was still missing, and the sadness she felt for the lost child had settled in on her like a half-frozen state of grief. She wanted to cry. But she knew it was not her loss, and even if it was, it wasn't exactly a loss. She was gone, just gone.

She'd awoken early and lay in her bed for an hour or more, unable to get back to sleep. Finally when she did, she'd fallen dead asleep, but not long enough to normally cycle back through a REM stage. When her alarm clock finally went off, she could hardly rouse herself from the drugged state. Somehow she made it in to the office, after barely managing to find an ensemble to wear, after what seemed like an hour of staring at her closet.

The atmosphere was just as drained. The trees had finally shed the last of their leaves. The overcast skies descended into a thick fog that completely blanketed the river valley, blotting out any views, even from Christine's condo windows. Everywhere she looked as she drove in she saw the same steel prison-wall gray. The river, she knew, flowed as always, but it too was hidden: whatever secrets it carried were even more concealed than usual by the heavy cover of fallen clouds. The conditions were so dangerous that visibility was less than a quarter mile. Flights coming into the nearest airport had been rerouted, and departing flights were delayed or cancelled. No one was going anywhere.

She'd just settled in to her desk when she looked up and saw Sharon peeking through a crack in the door. She didn't bother to ask, "What is it?" She merely looked up and waited.

Sharon came inside, closing the door quietly behind her, and practically tip-toeing over to the desk.

"It's the senator."

"Take a message, in fact, hold all my calls."

"She's not on the phone."

"Excuse me?"

"I said, she's not on the phone." Sharon stood waiting for Christine to understand. Then she quickly gave up. The woman simply had no patience.

"She's out there. In the waiting room," she mouthed, loud enough for Christine to hear.

"What's she doing here?" Christine asked.

Sharon shrugged her shoulders. "Like I would know? She asked to see you. She hopes she isn't interrupting anything."

"Tell her my schedule is full."

She knew Sharon would never do such a thing. Even if her schedule was full. Sharon hated things leaving things until "later." Now was just as good, in fact always better, than later.

"I scheduled her into your open slot. That means now."

Christine appreciated Sharon's efficiency. But she really thought it was time to find a new assistant.

"Give me a few minutes. I'll buzz you when I'm ready."

Sharon left, closing the door noiselessly behind her.

Christine put her hand on her phone, not because she was ready to buzz Sharon, but because she needed Arvo, even though she didn't want to need him. The skirmish inside pitted the logical against the emotional, with points for and against under each category. Arvo suspected the senator was involved in Abatha's disappearance in some way, and professionally she owed him the notice that the woman he'd wanted to interview was actually waiting in her office to speak with her.

She also wanted to gloat. Something he'd wanted but couldn't have was dropping in her lap. She would love to see his face as she triumphed in her catching the senator's attention, without even trying to. But wouldn't his presence distract her? She needed to grab whatever information she could from this visit and then report and glory over her victory later. The senator had, after all, not gone to see Arvo. She'd come to see Christine.

Still, as she buzzed Sharon, another part of her wished Arvo was there, and not just to witness her victory. She realized then she just wanted him. It was that simple.

Sharon ushered the senator in.

"Ms. Ivory," Senator Columbus-Powers said, striding across the room in a crisp navy suit and silk shirt. "I'm happy you had time to fit me into your schedule." Christine rose to accept the handshake. It was cool, firm and dry, professional and absolutely lacking in any personal warmth.

"Please, have a seat."'

"You have a beautiful view, Ms. Ivory, though with today's weather, unfortunately there's not much to see."

"Thank you, I enjoy it but rarely spend time looking out the window, Senator."

"Please, call me Jane. I'm not here on government business. It's personal."

Christine knew she wouldn't call the woman sitting across from her by something as intimate as a first name, not this woman anyway. And she didn't respond in that way. People needed to earn her intimacy. She realized Arvo took it without asking, and despite that violation, she had growing second thoughts about not letting him know who was visiting her.

"What is the personal business you want to see me about?"

"I have three daughters, aged nineteen, sixteen, and eleven. As the single mother of three daughters, I really want my girls to have every opportunity and use their potential the fullest. I'm sure you, as a professional woman, understand the special gifts girls have and how important it is to encourage them to be strong, courageous, and intelligent."

"I can understand the desire. Not having been particularly mentored myself, I'm not exactly sure what you're getting at."

"It's my middle daughter. Sarah. She's having some problems coping with things. I'm here to seek your help."

Christine knew she hadn't avoided raising her eyebrows at this personal request. What did this woman want from her? "I don't take private patients."

"Please don't refuse me right now. Please help a mother of a troubled daughter work through to some solution. I'm perhaps not completely aware of how the system works."

"I find that highly unlikely," Christine wished Arvo was watching this interchange. But of course he'd be butting in. "A person with your credentials is obviously aware of how the county government functions."

"Ms. Ivory, I am. I realize that this personal request may seem to be completely coming from out of left field. I'm actually trying to determine whether or not my daughter requires help. That's why I'm here."

"Only a professional working with her would know that. There are a number of diagnostic tools that would be employed—"

"Perhaps I'm being unclear," she smiled again. She was a master of making it appear that she truly was an unsure parent. "Please. Let me try again."

Christine was certain she had no interest in continuing the discussion. She had inquiries like this from other concerned parents all the time. And typically, she'd instantly turn them away. Getting involved in some personal family matter without the details, and without the authority to do so, was unethical. But she was convinced that the senator was in her office for an entirely different reason. It had already occurred to her that the senator was talking about a different daughter than the one they saw wearing the bracelet. Why this younger one? She was at least curious enough to allow the senator to continue her charade.

"I will. But let me remind you that I don't take private patients. And when I have these kinds of conversations with others, they never get to this point. I don't let it. There are ethical issues that prevent me from doing so."

"I understand. I will do my best to keep this at the level of two women discussing family life over coffee."

Christine knew that she was not the kind of person the senator would chum around with. She was fairly certain the senator didn't have girlfriends. That at least she shared with the senator: a professional life that superseded almost everything else.

"My daughter has suffered a tragic loss. I can't go into specifics, exactly, except to say that it is the kind of loss a girl of her age shouldn't experience. She's not the girl she used to be, it's like a part of her has run away. In fact, at times she has disappeared. We've tried to manage her, but everything we do fails."

Manage her? Even if one-tenth of what the senator was saying was true, she was sure that "managing" a child did nothing but push them away. "Without a lot of specifics, and I would ask you not to provide them, I really can't help you. The best I can do is refer you to a private psychologist who works with children. If you'll give me a moment, I'll get Sharon—"

"Christine. Please. I do think you can help me. A few more moments of your time." The senator looked down momentarily, then took a tissue from her pocket, wiping an unshed tear from the corner of her eye.

The level of false sincerity to the senator's tone was appalling. Christine was not sure how much more of the twisted performance she could take. The idea of delivering a message of triumph to Arvo had been quickly extinguished by her growing horror at what this woman might be capable of. Christine knew she was likely jumping to a premature conclusion, but she was convinced now that this woman had a role in Abatha's disappearance. And if that was the case, did it mean she had something to do with the poor baby's death? It took every ounce of her professionalism to keep from jumping over her desk and choking the woman.

"My daughter has lost something that's important to her. You know how children become attached to things. Maybe what she lost gave her some security in making that difficult transition children do when they are becoming an adult. It's a small trinket, really, of hardly any real value. I think you would recognize it if you saw it."

The senator paused to see the affect of her words on Christine. Christine gave her nothing but a determined expression. She knew the senator was talking about the bracelet. She knew she could say nothing, and only hope that the senator revealed more. Why was her older daughter wearing it? Was it the same one that Abatha had seen on the baby? How were the two bracelets connected, if at all? She knew enough, from working with the police, to keep quiet and let the interview go on. She had to.

"Well. Perhaps you can't tell me what I need to hear. Regardless. We've done everything to force the girl to look at certain realities. But she won't, and she's become even more withdrawn."

"I'm not sure I'm following you," Christine said vaguely, hoping the senator would slip and admit something.

"I'm being vague on purpose, to protect my daughter's privacy."

Which daughter's privacy, Christine wondered. "Again. The best I can offer you is a referral to someone else."

"I think you're missing my point. Ms. Ivory, I think you are well-positioned to help get what's missing back in its rightful place. You alone."

She stopped there and waited for again for a response from Christine. Christine finally found an answer to the revulsion threatening to overtake her. It flooded onto her face, making sharp edges on her that could not be mistaken for what she clearly felt: the deepest loathing for the woman sitting across from her.

The senator's mask slipped, revealing, momentarily, a cold hard expression. Christine clearly saw the hungry, grasping politician for what she was. A woman willing to do anything, including using her own children, to gain an advantage.

"Senator. There is nothing I can do for you. No, let me make that clearer. Even if I could do something for you, I wouldn't. I would never jeopardize my patients. I feel sympathy for your daughter, if indeed she is suffering. I hope she finds a way to get the help she needs, if and when she needs it."

Christine reached for her phone and the senator stopped her by placing her hand on top of Christine's. The fake maternal expression was again on the senator's face, but it wavered ever slightly, like a cold draft creeping in through a crack.

"You've forced me to do something I didn't want to. As a . . . mother, I am very protective and will do anything to keep my children out of harm's way. I know you can help me, Ms. Ivory. I'm convinced you have the power to make things happen, and I would show my appreciation if you did."

Was she offering to pay Christine? To do what? To make sure that as the senator revealed more, Christine wouldn't report her to the police? Christine was too dumbfounded to say anything.

"I also have power. Unlike yours, my power comes from years of bargaining and I can tell you I've built up a lot of chips that can be used both to appreciate people's helpful efforts and to provide consequences, when they are not so helpful."

"Are you threatening me?" Christine finally blurted.

The senator let go of her hand. Christine felt filthy, nauseated.

"Certainly not," she said, smiling, the face of the concerned parent taking hold once again in her expression. "I'm very sorry. This situation with my daughter, my concern for her welfare, has put me on edge. I apologize and I hope you understand. Someone with my years in the rough and tumble political world . . . I sometimes forget myself when I'm under stress. Again, I'm sorry if you felt threatened. I certainly didn't mean it."

Christine buzzed for Sharon, who immediately entered.

"Sharon, please give the senator a list of psychologists specializing in children. She's finished her discussion with me."

The senator stood up, wanting to say more but prevented by Sharon's presence in the room.

"I truly thank you for your time and expertise. We are grateful for any help you can offer in getting my daughter back to her normal self. We're not sure how much longer she can go on with this loss she's experienced."

As soon as Christine was sure the senator had left the building, she made her way down the elevator to Arvo's office.

"The senator just left my office . . ." she told him, out of breath. Then she felt her stomach churn and threaten. She'd forgotten to wash her hand. She ran out of Arvo's office, wondering if she'd have time to make it to the bathroom. She wretched into the sink, trying to stop the feeling by furiously soaping her hands. When she came back to Arvo's office, she noticed her knuckles were bleeding.

Christine relayed as much of the senator's conversation with her as quickly as she could. When she was finished, she wondered if he'd seen the tears of fury in her eyes.

"Did you see anyone following you when you came down here?" He said urgently.

"Arvo, you know I don't watch for that kind of thing. The only thing I could make sure of what that she was gone from the building before I made my way down here."

"That doesn't matter. She may have someone in the building. If that bracelet, for instance, was in evidence and somehow was stolen, it might have been an inside job. Someone could have been paid off. You need to start. Keep track of who you see."

"What does she want? Is she looking for Abatha? Doesn't she know where the girl is?"

"Maybe she found her and Abatha didn't have what she was looking for. I'm sorry to be so frank with you. No one has seen her yet. The trail is dead."

Christine quietly turned away. She didn't care now if he saw the tears in her eyes, but she didn't want to feel them, either. If she was looking at Arvo she wanted to see, clearly. And understand what she was being told.

"That's it?"

"I'm sorry."

"Isn't this enough to bring the senator in?"

"No."

Christine heard someone behind them. Arvo looked up.

"I've got something." It was Kieran. "Come to the lab."

"What's happening?" Juney said as they bustled by. Kieran gave her a look that made her jump out of her chair and quickly follow behind.

Camryn was standing next to Kieran's jumble of monitors and cables. Juney nearly tripped over a bundle of cords next to the doorway. "Are you people thinking of getting this place a little less cramped anytime soon?"

No one bothered answering her.

They gathered around Kieran's screen, which had been locked with a screensaver showing dancing Manga characters. He hit ctrl-alt-delete. Typed his password. Up came Riverbaby's Facebook page.

The daily status updates were much in character for her. The sights and sounds from a walk Kieran was taking for her, through twice a day phony Facebook updates.

"So. We see you've been keeping her up to date. You've been quite convincing. Keep it up."

"That's just the point. It is convincing, isn't it? But I can't take credit for something I haven't done. Not since yesterday, at least. "

"What are you saying?"

"I didn't update it today."

"But I see a status from 8:30 this morning."

"You are correct. Welcome to Facebook."

"Come on Kieran, spit it out," Juney said.

"I didn't put a status update in for her at 8:30 this morning. Someone else did."

They read it together. *Riverbaby . . . is with her best friend.*

"Camryn's trying to get a lock on the IP address associated with that entry."

"Text me as soon as you know something," Arvo said, his eyes on Christine. "Where are we going? You must know something about this best friend?"

"Yes. I know," she said, urging him along.

They left before Kieran had a chance to say anything else.

25

ARVO TOOK PAINS TO DRIVE A ROUTE that might allow them to proceed to their destination unnoticed. He'd considered borrowing Juney's ancient Mazda, but dismissed it realizing that if he needed horse-power, the lime-green compact wouldn't have a chance. He took the interstate following Christine's direction, weaving expertly in and out of traffic, but knew none of it mattered as soon as they exited.

"We're being followed."

Christine looked in the passenger side mirror to see if she could see who it was. "Did you recognize the car?"

"No. Get the plate number."

"I need something to write on," she said, her eyes on the mirror.

"You don't have your Blackberry?"

"Batteries dead."

"You, the over organized social worker? With a dead Blackberry? Unbelievable." Arvo squealed onto a side street. "You should know that there are plenty of scraps of paper in my glove compartment." He reached over and popped it open, his eyes never leaving the road. "Be my guest."

Christine found a scrap and a stub of a pencil. "It looks like a rental car."

"Write that down."

"I can just make out most of the plate."

Arvo flipped open his cell phone and hit the redial button. "Juney, we have a plate we need run. Also, check in with Kieran. Any luck on that IP Address yet?"

He handed Christine the phone and she read off the numbers and the rental company name. She handed the phone back.

"Yes, I know it takes time to get through to the rental companies. So get going."

They turned into the school parking lot and the car following them cruised on by before they could see who was driving.

They headed inside to find Mr. Shenouda, and learned he was at work in the temporary office.

"Let me handle this, Arvo."

"Fine." Arvo excused himself. "I'll keep tabs on our friend. Maybe he has some educational needs."

"I wasn't aware that you would be coming today," Mr. Shenouda said, excusing himself. "I'll finish later." He began to gather up his cleaning supplies. Christine noticed the improvement in the room.

"Mr. Shenouda, actually I came to speak with you. Would you mind?" She pointed to a chair. "Please sit down."

She pulled the desk chair around and sat near him without being too intrusive.

"Mr. Shenouda, I know that you and Abatha are close."

Mr. Shenouda nodded slightly, a stern look on his face.

"She's a special girl and I want you to know that both I, and Detective Thorson, are doing all we can to make sure she's safe."

"Yes." Mr. Shenouda's eyes lit up, but the stern expression remained. "The child has a special place . . ."

Christine's eyes began to fill with tears. She cleared her throat. "I . . . I have been devastated since I learned of her disappearance. I have many patients, Mr. Shenouda, many patients. So many of them are fragile and special, and in order to give them what they need, I need to maintain a distance. It's the most important thing I can do. I need to be completely honest with them in order to give them a picture they themselves can't see."

Mr. Shenouda listened carefully. Christine felt he was forming a picture of her. She wondered what he was seeing.

"When I become too close, it can jeopardize their health. Because when I get too close, the treatment focus may shift. To me. My issues. Instead of theirs."

Christine felt her throat ache. She cleared her throat again. "I'm sorry, I really meant to ask you something, rather than explain myself."

"Please," Mr. Shenouda said, the sternness unchanged though his eyes were brighter, "tell me what you need to tell me."

"I've been completely unable to focus on my patients this past few weeks. I have gotten too close to a patient of mine, and not only is it potentially preventing me from giving my other patients what they need, it also may jeopardize this patient. Unfortunately, I'm stuck. I can't stop thinking about Abatha. I'm completely beside myself with worry over her."

Mr. Shenouda watched her.

"I'm terribly sorry for burdening you with my feelings. This is not what I came to . . . tell you."

Mr. Shenouda put one of his small, strong hands on hers. "I'm glad you came to tell me what you have. If there was a way I could put you at some ease, I would. No one worries about that child more than I do." His eyes sharpened like an eagle's. He looked out the window, and Christine could see he was nearly overcome himself. He was considering something in the distance.

"Thank you for understanding. Do you . . . can you tell me anything that will help with the investigation. I'm so afraid for her. I can't sleep. I can't think."

Mr. Shenouda grasped her hand and the eagle-sharp eyes looked around him. He got up for a moment, walked over and closed the door, then sat down next to Christine again, taking her hands in his.

"Ms. Ivory, I'll tell you something and I hope you can believe me when I say it." Mr. Shenouda went on. "I have seen terrible things happen to children. Neglect. Violence. Poverty. Many times I have not been able to do anything but watch."

He patted her hand then briefly eyed a distant spot out the window.

"This time I am also watching. I'm watching over. I assure you—no harm will come to that child. I know it and you can know it. Please," he said, both hands on hers, "Abatha would not want you worried over her, not in this way."

Christine pulled his hands up to her face, sobbing in relief, not knowing how else to thank Mr. Shenouda. He would say no more than what he had, she knew it. She wished he could admit it baldly, but he couldn't. That might endanger her more than she already was.

"I have something for her," Christine finally was able to say, "For when you next see her. And I hope that will be very soon."

"Please, I will keep it for her. What is it?"

Christine opened her purse and found a folded piece of paper. The senator and her oldest daughter in their ball gowns.

"If you would keep this for her, and when you see her sometime, please show it to her."

The janitor took the paper, folded it, and placed it in his breast pocket. He patted his hand on it. "I won't forget what you've asked."

Mr. Shenouda pushed his cart out of the room, bowed his head slightly, then left her by herself. Moments later, Arvo was standing in the doorway. He watched her, then came to her, taking her in his arms quietly while she sobbed. She knew she was ruining her makeup, and she hadn't seen a mirror since the early morning. She didn't care.

When she had finally quieted, Arvo tipped her face up to learn what it was she knew. The dark circles were still under her eyes, the concealer had washed away to reveal the truth of her feelings. Her eyes were red. Still, they told him what they had both hoped would be true about the girl's safety. Was Mr. Shenouda telling the truth? Or wishing desperately for what they searched for, but feared they might not find? They didn't know him as well as Abatha did.

"We need to get back, Christine. Kieran's still working on that IP Address, Juney's chasing down the guy following us. If he's still out there, we need to give him someone to follow. He needs to be led away from here, in particular."

They drove back in silence, taking the road along the river. They slowed by the road leading under the railroad tracks. Looking up, they sought an answer about which direction to go.

High above the river, eagles sat in a treetop, and as they came to the intersection, they spread their wings and were lifted in the currents of air heated by the bright autumn sun that had finally reappeared that afternoon.

They headed back to the office, noting that their escort had disappeared. When they arrived in the office, Juney and Kieran were standing together, waiting for them.

"Another update?"

Kieran answered by leading them down the hallway into the crowded computer lab. Camryn got up from her desk, too, eager to get away from the Internet pornography case she was looking into.

"Well? What do you have for us, Kieran?"

He hit ctrl-alt-delete and tapped in his password. Riverbaby's Facebook page popped up, and they held their collective breath as they all read the lines.

Riverbaby sees the bracelet. Again.

Juney handed him a paper. "Something else came in while you were away." She handed Arvo a manila envelope from an out-of-state lab the office used for evaluating DNA. Arvo opened the envelope and removed the detailed report. The first several pages were all procedural, validating the sterile collection of the evidence, certifying the chain of control. Arvo almost lost his patience.

"Where is it, Juney? You know I hate paperwork."

She took the pages back and flipped to the part she knew he wanted to see.

"Do you see what I see?"

"Related? To the older case? How is that even possible?"

"Everything's always possible, Arvo."

"That tells me you have something else. What now?"

"We have the info on who has the rental. Does the name Jakob Masaryk mean anything to you?"

"That confirms what we suspected. Get me a phone number for the guy. By the way he keeps following me around, he obviously wants a date."

Juney gave him her irritated look, as if to say, are you accusing me of not being thorough? "It's at my desk."

"Wait a minute. Something else just happened to Abatha's page."

Everyone turned back to his monitor. Kieran took the mouse cursor and pointed to a comment that had just come in on her page.

Mississippiboi? "The guy sure moves fast."

Mississippiboi sees a silver bracelet, too.

Arvo took a sharp breath and swung into action. "Juney—get the sheriff up to speed. Tell him to round up a posse. I'll check in later to give him the time and the place."

"Sure, boss."

"By the way . . ." he took her aside, speaking in confidence. "Get in touch with Internal Affairs. There's a leak, somewhere in the coroner's department. They better get it plugged up really fast. I'm not going to do their job for them, but they might want to check into the bank statements for the past couple of months.

Large transactions either way. I'd say we have someone with a money problem in need of a lot of cash, fast, and with a sense for the jewelry, especially silver jewelry."

Juney's eyes blazed. "You don't have to tell me twice. I hate someone messing with my nice, tidy evidence files even more than I hate a snitch."

26

ARVO HAD NO PROBLEM ARRANGING a meeting with Masaryk. The man was in a hurry to unload whatever he had acquired. This meant that Masaryk was also closer than he had ever been to making a misstep, since most likely Arvo wasn't the only person seeking what the Slovakian had in his possession. Having tipped Juney to the location where he planned to meet Masaryk, he calculated the precise amount of time it would take for the sheriff to gather and have in place the assorted legal and law enforcement types that would track this aider and abettor to the crime, and any other potential suspects, witnesses, and perpetrators. He wished he had twice as much time, but knew he couldn't chance Masaryk changing his mind, or the real murderer getting away.

Arvo entered the posh downtown restaurant casually, the wireless microphone concealed in his pocket, even the earpiece unremarkable as it was housed simply in his cell phone. He'd completed his testing of the device as he left his car, signing off to Kieran when he closed his car door. He'd noted the locations of the half-dozen unmarked squads, and acknowledged, almost imperceptibly, the hostess, an undercover who'd been in place for years at the grill. The Downtowner had long been a convenient location of the discreet busts of the cream of high society in these parts. It had seen its share of perp walks over the years, from financial scandals to sex crimes. No one was too rich or too powerful to be connected to an arrest here. Chet Freeman, the proprietor, loved the publicity he got whenever an arrest was made and he made sure he was in the shot when the cameras showed up out front. The Downtowner's notoriety had been sealed since the early 1970s, when a shoot out between the police and a sleazy drifting serial murderer calling himself Clyde Bonnie left the tin ceilings and paneled walls punched through with bullet holes. Chet just gathered the empty shell cases to sell to curiosity seekers, and accented the bullet holes with glow in the dark paint.

Though if the restaurant really did have a conscience, or a sense of humility, it might be ashamed that today's victim was such a small potato as Masaryk, who was waiting, unknowing, at his table.

Arvo could see that the man was eager to bargain. And that he was nervous.

"I'm being watched," he said, his eyes darting around the room.

"By who?" Arvo said nonchalantly.

"The senator. I recognize her security people."

"Is that so?"

"Can you help me?"

"Depends," Arvo answered. "On whether you can help me."

Masaryk reached into his pocket and got out his worn leather wallet. He set it on the table and opened it. In it, Arvo saw the fine, fragile silver bracelet. Masaryk flicked a small charm, a dangling heart that hung from the end of it. On the back Arvo read a name inscribed on it. It was the name of the senator's eldest daughter.

"How is it a big guy like you came across a little thing like that? That doesn't look like your style, Masaryk."

Masaryk snapped the wallet closed with his giant palm. His thick, hairy wrist concealed the little bracelet without much effort.

"You mentioned a win-win situation, Detective? I've been cheated by a very powerful woman, a senator. She made a number of promises to me, none of which she kept. I'm prepared to give you what you need, if I can get what I need."

"First I need to confirm that this is what I've been looking for. To do that, I need to know how you came to find it."

"Do you think me stupid, Detective?"

"You're a business man, Masaryk. You know the difference between buying something genuine and a cheap replica. No deal until you show me that you know the difference."

Masaryk eyed the person he recognized watching him from the corner of the restaurant.

"It came from the arm of an infant washed up on the river shore, not too long ago. A girl found the baby. It's been in all the newspapers."

"And how do you, YOU, know that this is the same bracelet that was on that baby's arm."

Masaryk gave a nervous laugh.

"Why? Because I took it from the official who recovered it from the poor baby's arm. I saw for myself a need to be able to authenticate everything, and be able to get the highest price possible from the person who was so anxious to have the piece of jewelry returned. I watched."

Arvo's gut boiled and his fists tightened. He knew enough to appear calm. Masaryk seemed to need no encouragement to continue.

"This was not long before we first met, Mr. Thorson. You see I am not the only person who learns quickly the value of these things. Everyone will bargain. Everyone has a price point. A good businessman knows how to prepare himself, thoughtfully, to get the greatest return. And to what lengths one must sometimes go. The official in the coroner's department was not too difficult to bargain with, though the man is a gambler, and not a very good one."

Arvo tried to keep his face from showing the disgust he really felt. "It sounds as if negotiations may have broken down with the party you intend to sell to?"

"Sadly. Yes. I had thought of working with the opponent of my customer. My calls were not returned. Your American politics, does, sometimes, maintain a high ethic. Sometimes."

"Not looking for a new buyer?"

"No. I am, what's the phrase, 'cutting my losses.' Now that the girl has disappeared. The senator has ceased all negotiations with me. "

Arvo had heard all he needed, Kieran's voice confirming it in his ear. He signaled by scratching under his arm and instantly Masaryk was surrounded by a dozen undercover police, who quickly cuffed him.

The senator's man across the room was quickly surrounded by other police officers, all dressed as restaurant patrons, though had he actually succeeded in making it to any of the restaurant doors, he'd have found his way barred. The undercover hostess had hit a hidden button under her stand that instantly sealed all of the exits.

Arvo hurried through the arrest process, knowing that there was very little time left: Abatha's whereabouts were still unknown. He jumped in his car, and sped to the senator's campaign headquarters. He knew he should call in for back up, but was afraid of tipping the senator off. Who knew what inside connections, even insiders from the county, might alert her. She had the power and resources to get away, despite her high profile. She'd proven she would use that power, any way and any time she wanted, to get whatever she wanted, no matter the danger or the personal cost, even to her own flesh and blood. A woman who was capable of murdering her own grandchild and her own child would stop at nothing.

Arvo rushed into the storefront campaign headquarters where a dozen staffers were slouched over phones, making pitches to contributors.

"I need to see the senator," he said to a man he recognized from the event at Abatha's school.

"The senator doesn't see anyone without an appointment."

Arvo flipped open his badge. "This is my appointment." He walked through the room searching for the senator and spotted an office door at the back of the room with the senator's name on it. He rushed to it, and rattled the knob only to find the door was locked.

He banged on the door. "Open up, it's the police." He pounded on the door, then grabbed the nearest chair and began slamming it into the door. It exploded into a useless pile of junk and Arvo spotted the next best thing, a desk. He pushed a worker aside, and smashed the heavy steel desk against the door like a battering ram.

The campaign worker screamed and another man shouted "You can't do this! This is outrageous!" Workers began to quickly exit the room. As Arvo was pulling the desk back to prepare for another go at the door, the man with the ear piece hustled up, inserting himself between Arvo and the door.

"Sir, you have no authority to come barging in here without a warrant."

"Look, pal, I'm warning you. Get out of my way before we both regret it. Well maybe you more than me," he panted hoarsely.

A man near the front door shouted, "I'm calling the police."

Arvo answered, "I am the God damned police. Now move aside."

Arvo heard a door fly open from inside the senator's office, then the heavy thud of a car door slamming in the parking lot next to the building. An engine roared to life and car tires squealed.

Arvo finally succeeded in pushing his way past the ear-piece wearing man, and crashing through the door with a blocking move he hadn't made in over twenty years. His sore shoulder reminded him why. He rushed through, only to see the senator speeding away in her BMW. He raced out just as Christine pulled up.

"Get in." They screeched off with Christine at the wheel. "Juney told me where to find you."

"I don't like it when I'm not in control of the steering wheel," Arvo said

"It's my turn to drive. Just keep an eye on her. And buckle up, I'm a reckless driver. Especially when I drive fast."

They closed in on the senator, Christine competently taking the sharp turns, but her high mileage, earth-friendly compact was no match for the BMW: the moment they seemed to closed in, she pulled away. Christine heard Arvo requesting back up.

"Nothing against your driving. I'm actually impressed," he said. Ahead, in the senator's car, Arvo saw a weapon pointing at them out the back window.

"She's not alone!" Christine shouted as she swerved and a shot blew off the passenger side mirror. Arvo cranked down the passenger side window and positioned his revolver.

"We'll show her what a couple of her constituents really think of her." He fired back, aiming for the rear tires, but narrowly missing as the senator's car swung off the highway to take the dirt road to the swing bridge.

"The bridge is closed for repair, isn't it?" Arvo shouted over the noise. A gun shot from the senator's car hit the gravel in front of them, spitting rocks that ricocheted off the front grill. Arvo returned the fire.

"I guess we'll find out," Christine said, "and just hope barge traffic isn't coming through."

The senator's car crashed through a construction barrier, and Christine swiftly followed, bumping over the crushed warning signs. They hit the bridge deck just as the lights began to flash and horns began clanging. Arvo glanced down river and saw a flotilla of barges heading their way, the tug boat blaring its horn. "Well doesn't that just suck," he said. Christine swore.

Barrier gates closed fifty yards in front of the senator's car, and she raced ahead anyway. Arvo saw Christine responding, her speedometer needle rising past seventy, then eighty miles an hour. The senator broke through the gates, the blow causing her car to careen briefly, then she sped up again and flew across the stretch of swing deck. Beneath them, Christine and Arvo felt the swing section rumbling to life and the old deck creaking an unearthly sound in preparation for the bridge to swivel open.

The senator's car made it to the gates on the far end of the swing section, crashing through, the impact this time causing her car to veer and graze a side rail. A gap opened between the swing section and the eastern deck and Christine gunned her engine, launching her car over the widening gap. They were airborne for a few heart-stopping moments, until the car slammed down on the opposite side, the rear tires hitting the edge of the open gap, with no space to spare and nothing but the river below. She lost control of the car as it pitched sideways and nearly began to roll, but quickly managed to right herself.

In a matter of seconds they were off the bridge and chasing the senator near the entrance to the gasoline refinery. Arvo aimed quickly and shot out one of the senator's rear tires, causing her to spin out. As soon as she could, she hit the gas again, heading straight through the entrance to the refinery.

"Shoot her again," Christine yelled over the sound of the roaring engine.

"What, and blow us all up?" Arvo said.

Shots were fired in their direction. A section of pipeline was hit, spilling a flammable substance onto the roadway in front of them, which immediately erupted into flames.

"So she's going to kill us instead then?"

"Suit yourself, Ms Know it all," Arvo said, taking careful aim at the senator's car again. He held his fire as the car disappeared behind a fuel tank. Christine made a sharp turn, her car swinging 180 degrees. She righted herself and closed in on the senator. Arvo aimed and blew out another tire. This time, the senator's car spun completely out of control and rolled over, tumbling off the roadway directly into a fuel tank.

Christine hit the brakes and Arvo leapt out of the car.

"Arvo, don't . . . it could explode!"

Flames shot from a shattered pipe. The fire spread quickly along the passenger side of the car, where the senator's passenger had partially ejected out the back window, gruesomely broken and still. Arvo reached the car and wrenched the battered door open, quickly unbuckling the unconscious senator from her car seat and tugging her out of the car.

He hauled her away from the perilously spreading fire, dragged her to Christine's car, where she quickly helped him to get her inside. Arvo jumped into the driver's seat and tore away as the senator's car became completely engulfed and a throaty growl sounded from deep within the fuel tank. As Arvo raced full speed to get away, Christine turned to watch it explode, sending fiery, deadly plumes a quarter mile into the air. Moments later, police cars and fire trucks screamed by as Arvo and Christine exited the refinery complex and pulled over by the side of the road. The senator moaned from her back seat, still alive, then struggled to sit up, coughing.

"You're under arrest," Arvo told her, "for murder." A squad pulled up alongside of Arvo as he read her the rest of her rights. The woman broke down when she realized what her shame and ambition had lost her.

In the days that followed her arrest, a horrific story was pieced together of how years earlier, she'd become pregnant while still unmarried. This inconvenient and unwanted baby gave her no other option. She dreaded the judgment of her father, and saw for herself only years of shame and rejection were she to either seek abortion, adoption, or raise the child herself. The years of achievement and steady accumulation of power and wealth hadn't really ever validated that first, secret, heinous murder of her own child. And when that influence she'd worked so hard to achieve began to wane, the senator learned her own unmarried daughter had a secret that, were it known, would completely undo everything she stood for. She knew she couldn't keep her promise to her daughter, to quietly seek adoption for the baby. So she hid its birth and hoped she'd erased its death in the same river grave where she had lain her firstborn, over twenty years earlier. In her haste to dispose of the baby, she hadn't noticed the tiny, silver bracelet her crying daughter had put around her child's wrist. A remembrance from her young mother, who would never forget the loss of her first born.

But the river kept no one's secrets, the seasons saw to that. This time was no different. The river never forgets. Its power is in always revealing everything it touches, in telling everything it knows.

Thorson took care of the paperwork as quickly as he could, though it in fact took hours to make all the statements, file all the reports, and face the cameras as the county sheriff made his statements.

"Yes. The two babies are related, according to the DNA evidence," the sheriff answered. "We won't be able to confirm definitively the possible relation between the babies and the senator for a few weeks, but we expect that work will only corroborate the statements we have taken already from the senator's daughter and other individuals now in custody." Thankfully, it was the sheriff who took care of the press. He knew Arvo had important work to finish. Arvo would want the case to be airtight.

There really was, however, only one loose end that needed to be wrapped up in order for Arvo to be completely satisfied. This task was checked off his to-do list at approximately 7:30 p.m. the night Masaryk and the soon to be ex-senator, Jane Columbus-Powers, were locked into the Mendota County jail.

Christine stood in the doorway of Thorson's office, and he looked at her with a hopeful expression. She was beaming. "She's okay, Arvo. She's at home with her grandmother."

He quickly took Christine into his arms, and she released her tears at first into his shoulder. He tipped up her face and saw her beautiful face releasing, with abandon, all the genuine passion she'd held quietly within.

Arvo pulled Christine into his office, and closed and locked his office door—Juney could wait for another half an hour until he turned over his reports to her.

27

CHRISTINE WAITED IN HER SOMERSET Hills middle school office. She had infrequently visited over the past month, and once the New Year arrived in just a few weeks, the office would be closed permanently and renovated into a special programs room under Christine's direction. Christine had secured a grant and designed a unique service to provide at-risk children the emotional and social support they needed to succeed academically. After the first of the year, she'd get the chance to help children like Abatha, children who might not otherwise even be noticed except for a dreadful circumstance. Working with Abatha had spurred Christine to think hard about how better to serve gifted children like her, before, rather than after a tragedy. As a result, Eagle Aerie for Kids would be opening for business soon.

She got up from the desk and took a quick look around the room, noting nothing at all was out of place. It was spotless. It had been for the past two months, carefully repaired, painted, and equipped by Mr. Shenouda. When he'd revealed why and how it had come about that he provided Abatha her safe haven, and it was clear that Abatha's grandmother had no complaints or concerns with his action, any potential kidnapping charges were quickly dropped. In fact, the janitor had been made a hero by the press. His quick thinking saved Abatha's life.

Behind her on the credenza that she and Abatha had cleared off so long ago, Christmas cards made by schoolchildren were festively on display. Outside the window, the distant refinery twinkled in the near solstice waning daylight. Snow fell in thick clumps.

Christine heard a knock on the office door, and she stood and smoothed out the floral sweater dress she wore and absently fingered the smooth natural waves in her loose hair, which had been dyed back to its normal rich brown color.

She opened the door and there stood Mr. Shenouda. He stepped aside, revealing Abatha, holding a tiny poinsettia plant.

"You got this for me?" she said.

Abatha giggled. "No, I'm just the delivery girl." She looked to the hallway, at someone, out of Christine's view.

A smile broadened across Christine's face, and she said loudly, "I didn't think you were the kind of guy who went in for this kind of thing. I mean, flowers? For a girl?"

"I guess you don't know me as well as you think," Arvo said, stepping inside.

"Well, aren't you looking cheery, Mr. Christmas elf," she told him. And he did. He looked healthier and happier than he'd been in a long time. He had been immediately reinstated, with full back pay and a clean record, after the arrests. He still had dark days, and expected to have them to come. But they seemed less frequent, not quite as deep, and when he got to the other side of them, life seemed smoother, like calm water after a brief storm. He hoped the trend would continue.

"Come on," he said, gesturing with exaggerated arm movements to everyone that it was time to leave. "What about that lunch you promised us?"

"I think you weren't invited? Right Abatha? Just us girls?" Christine winked.

"What if I promised to do some Christmas caroling? Down at the shelter? I've been practicing," Arvo said, belting out "O Christmas Tree."

"Stop!" Christine laughed. "Stop!"

He only got louder and more off key.

She howled, "Uncle! I give up. Lunch for everyone on me."

He mercifully stopped. "Okay. Thank you for inviting me." He helped Christine into her lime-green, cashmere-lined leather jacket. She grabbed her coordinated purse, and glanced at a mirror to check her makeup.

Some things never changed.

Arvo held the door as everyone headed out. Before he closed it, he took one final look out the window to see the refinery looming across the river, its bright fires flaring and smoking, and the river frozen under a fresh blanket of snow.

ACKNOWLEDGEMENTS

I am indebted to my writing group — Melissa Doffing, Anika Fajardo, and Lindsay Taylor — for the feedback and encouragement they provided over the years. The many times I felt like quitting, they were quick with a motivating word. When I asked for help from my writing group, I always got the help I needed.

So now it's my turn to pay it forward.

I am very thankful to Mary Pat Lee, executive director of the Greater Minneapolis Crisis Nursery, the first of its kind in Minnesota. In giving me a tour through the facility, she emphasized the critical importance of providing a safe haven for at-risk young children and support for parents (most often mothers) in crisis.

While the Crisis Nursery sheltered more than 2,000 children in 2009, it was forced to turn away twice as many children as it could place. Without support and services, the result can be grim. During 2009 in Minnesota, almost 4,742 children were the victims of abuse and neglect, and of those, 44 suffered life-threatening injuries and 21 died from maltreatment (www.dhs.state.mn.us).

With such so much at stake and stretched resources, Mary Pat Lee told me that her advocates' only goal at times is to teach stressed parents how to ask for help. For many, asking for help is a huge step towards improving their family's lives. But when the call for help is made, and no help is available, consequences can be dire.

Therefore, on the Crisis Nursery's behalf, I hope readers of Washed Up can help in supporting the Crisis Nursery's mission – so that when a parent takes that important and very scary first step, there are available services to meet their needs.

Please check the Minneapolis Crisis Nursery's website (www.crisisnursery.org) and provide the support you can, or reach out to your local Crisis Nursery to see how you can help.

BOOK GROUP DISCUSSION GUIDE

1. Washed Up opens with the discovery of the worst crime most of us can imagine: an innocent infant has been murdered. How did the crime affect you? Did you wonder if you could read a book about the murder of a baby?

2. In a period from the late 1990's to the early 2000's three drowned babies (two of whom were determined to be related) have been discovered near Red Wing, Minnesota. The author has been haunted for years by these very real crimes, and this prompted her to write Washed Up. Some consider the murder of infants taboo as a mystery subject. Are there novel topics that should be considered taboo? Why?

3. The setting of the book is based on the area where the author grew up; however, she fictionalized the county and city names. How would the book have been different for you had the setting been the actual location, either the author's home town or Red Wing, Minnesota?

4. How affected are you by novels set in places familiar to you? How does the story location affect your interest in a novel? Are you more interested in reading about 'faraway' places? What does reading about a place like home do for you?

5. The novel followed, for the most part, a typical 'three-act' structure. Very simply: the first part included the 'set up,' opening with the discovery of a body, introducing characters, and setting up conflicts; the second part is maze-like – characters keep ending up in dead-ends, tensions grow; the third part is climax-resolution-dénouement (or closure). How closely did the three acts align with the three parts of the novel? How did the structure help you (or not) as a reader?

6. The river played a very symbolic role in the novel. In what way did the river's 'mood' parallel the story arc? How did setting, as a whole, function in the novel?

7. Arvo Thorson has spent his entire life in Somerset Hills. Christine Ivory returned to it after some time away. Does living in their hometown signal a resignation? Why or why not?

8. Pretend you are a foreigner and one of your early experiences of Minnesota culture comes to you through reading Washed Up (translated, of course, into your native tongue). What do you discover about the Midwest by reading Washed Up? How does the local culture shape the story?

9. Both Arvo and Christine are at the mid-point of their careers, and their lives. How does their stage of life contribute to their conflicts with other characters? And each other?

10. Christine Ivory is a strong female character: a professional woman with her own unique sense of style. How important is it to you to read about strong female characters? In the end, she succumbs to Arvo's charms (such as they are). Does she still seem like a strong woman, even in her weak moments?

11. The other strong woman character in the novel is the villain. She has no redeeming value. Do you believe in evil? That there are real, evil people in the world? Why or why not?